THRESHOLD

a novel

Andy Lockwood

ISBN: 978-1628282252 eBook
ISBN: 978-1628282245 Paperback

Cover Illustration and Design by Brian Ritson

This is a work of fiction. Names, characters, places, and incidents are either products of the author's imagination or are used fictitiously and are not to be construed as real. Any resemblance to actual people, living or dead, or to businesses, organizations, events, institutions, or locales, is purely coincidental.

Woe be upon anyone who steals, or borrows and does not return, this book from its owner. May ink from the page stain the thief's hands, marking them for all to see. Let the ink burn, words marking their skin for all time. Let bookworms crawl under their fingertips, burrowing a home where they will gnaw like guilt and shame.

Published by Just Ducky Editing 2020

Other books by Andy Lockwood:

Empty Hallways

House of Thirteen, Book One

At Calendar's End

…because I never thought I'd find the ending.

…because I had to wrestle time, depression, and myself to finish it.

…because the person who started it never got here, and the person who got here is still amazed he made it.

This one is for me.

"Mirrors,' she said, 'are never to be trusted."

-   Neil Gaiman, *Coraline*

PROLOGUE

Harriet sat in her favorite chair, watching the sun descend through the trees outside. She raised her glass absently, red wine ebbing back and forth in the glass, as she attempted to recall memories associated with each glass from her past. She swirled the remnants around, the gentle motion hypnotic. Memories rose like ghosts behind her eyes, reflecting on the life she'd led to this point.

It was, without doubt, a good, long life, full of adventure – certainly longer than anyone would have bet on. Harriet was not one to mind her tongue nor shy from confrontation. She'd led volunteer rescue efforts through hurricanes and raced tornadoes till they ran out of breath. Harriet had loved some unlovable men and hated others right into their graves. She succeeded and failed with so many businesses that she couldn't remember all the jobs she knew how to do. Her family called her fearless, but that wasn't quite it. Harriet understood when fear was foolhardy and when it was an appropriate response.

As many times as she recalled all of her adventures to family and friends, she never wrote them down. There was no history of her escapades, save the one shared with her grandchildren over the years. Perhaps Catherine, her most ambitious grandchild, would collect the stories in a memoir. Catherine had threatened as much, but she had the same fire as her grandmother. Both Cate and Harriet were so full of want-to-do and lacking when-it's-time that neither were sure it would ever happen. Harriet hoped it would, but knew that she would not be around to see it realized.

For the last year, she'd been increasingly aware of a wooziness that overcame her during the day. In the beginning, it was infrequent; a mere blip on life's radar. But as the frequency increased, it became apparent that this was not a condition to be ignored. It was time to call the doctor.

Even when the appointment was scheduled, the worry lingered far outside her rational thoughts. As far as Harriet was concerned, Death was a point on an ever-expanding timeline, and she would extend that point as far out as she was capable.

Her doctor seemed more surprised than she was with the diagnosis. Hypertrophic cardiomyopathy, he called it. Harriet hated medical terminology. It twisted her tongue into confusion and made her head hurt trying to translate the garbage.

"Something's wrong with my heart." She repeated in the same slow and patient tone she used on her grandchildren when they were young and frustrated with the world. "I know that. That's what I came to you for."

He explained that her heart was not pumping the way it should, and the best plan of action was to begin medication while they discussed options for prolonging her life – or planning for the eventual end.

She listened to the explanation. She sat patiently and nodded when it was appropriate. He was a smart, young doctor and didn't need to be discouraged. When he was done providing assurances, she decided that it would be best to spend her remaining days at home in relative comfort. She didn't need hospice, nor did she need to concern her family over the issue.

Yes, she told him, she understood the choice she was making. You didn't reach ninety-one without understanding the inherent risks of living. You also didn't reach ninety-one expecting to escape them. Her mind was set: getting to the end at her own comfortable pace without a perpetual reminder of her own dwindling mortality. Sense and science be damned, Harriet wanted to die happy and without complication.

So far, tomorrow always managed to arrive. With each passing day, her trepidation eased, and she began to understand that this opportunity had been given to her as a gift, one that would not be squandered. Each day was spent deliberately, doing the things she wanted to do – things she wanted to enjoy one last time. She set out to make each moment count and hoped that these lessons would be passed on to those she left behind.

Harriet absently drew rings with the base of the glass, listening to the hypnotic song of the glass ringing softly against the fabric. Draining the last of the wine, she left the empty glass on her side table. Standing slowly, she made her way to the bedroom to prepare for bed. She smiled at the pictures on the walls, familiar faces and memories smiling back at her as she inched closer to the bedroom. Harriet wondered to herself who would look after her possessions when she was gone: what houses they would occupy next, and in whose minds her memories would dwell after they'd left her. She hoped that all of her things would go to people who deserved them; people who would look after them, caring for them with the same affection she did.

Crossing the doorway into her bedroom, Harriet's smile faded with each progressive step. Her mouth dipped low as she scowled at the mirror in the corner. The scowl was as much a part of her nightly routine as her nightgown. As each night before, she regarded the antique with the same disdain as a child that knowingly disregarded the house rules.

She glared at the monstrosity, the lone exception among her cherished belongings. She hoped that wherever it wound up, it would have a long life neglected and forgotten, collecting dust in disuse for the rest of time.

Harriet stared at it and found herself drifting closer with each step. The force, though waning, was still enough that it could not be mistaken for her own volition. It surprised her that after all this time, it still had the power to try drawing her in. She let it bring her closer still, approaching the corner of her bed. Putting a hand out, thin fingers closed around the post of the footboard, squeezing gently to anchor her.

Her eyes traced the intricate designs carved into the wooden frame, still wondering who had carved them and whether they held any significance to the mirror's nature.

She felt drawn to stand in front of the glass. That was where it wanted her. It was a gentle nudge now, but she remembered how insistent it used to be. Had Harriet not been the bold force of nature she was, things might have turned out differently between herself and the looking glass. It was possible she would have more answers if she'd given in. It was also possible that those answers would have cost her years, or even her life. She never gave it what it wanted, always finding some way to dodge its call and deny its hunger. She snubbed it satisfaction as it refused her answers. Even though she had come out ahead, she felt cheated.

For a handful of years, her focus had been on seeking answers about the mirror. There were none – at least as far as she had discovered. Local antiquarians made guesses; amateur woodcrafters stumbled through explanations. Even when Catherine showed her how to search the internet, Harriet could find nothing but scant rumors.

It eluded her, so in retaliation, she eluded it.

Her arm swayed in and out of the very edge of the visible reflection. The rest of her remained comfortably in obscurity. Her arm rocked again, drifting further into the frame. The muscles in her back flexed as if she might lean forward. She could feel herself being pulled again toward the reflection. It was a gentle insistence, like the weight of water pressing in when she did laps at the pool. Her grip tightened on the bedpost; it wasn't much, but enough to bring her back to the present and reset her resolve.

"You know well enough by now; I'm not going to give in."

One last time, she felt a tug, harder than before. Still, she held firmly to the post in the event that she pitched too far forward as she rocked gently.

Of all the things Harriet had accomplished in her life – and the feats were innumerable – she was always disappointed that she'd never dug up any answers about her damned artifact. No manufacturer, no previous owners, no guesses – reasonable or otherwise – on how old it was. It seemed that the harder she looked, the less she was able to find… or remember. Even her own memory of acquiring it was obscured. She vaguely remembered when she got it – she won an auction. It had been a spur of the moment impulse – a rebound purchase to help her adjust to life after her husband's passing. Jake would have scoffed at the idea of such a thing in their home, so she had to have it. Harriet won the auction, paid for the mirror, and it had been delivered. She couldn't remember anything else about it and wondered now if that had been its doing all along. How many interactions could she not recall because it wouldn't let her? There were plenty of moments her family had chalked up to senility that Harriet was questioning now. Had she always been accepting of it – or was she only now becoming immune to its power?

Harriet considered many times reaching outside her community for explanations about the mirror, but in the end, couldn't bring herself to it. The more people she let in on her secret, the less control she had over it. With time came further obscurity, and the hope for answers dwindled. Instead, Harriet focused on keeping it away from anyone else for fear of what might happen.

More than once, she considered destroying the thing. Even fewer times, she acted on the notion. While it lacked the power – or desire, Harriet could never tell – to draw her in, it made up for that with its ability to defend itself. Harriet could barely touch it; it knew if she planned to threaten it – even the smallest offense. She pressed her thumbnail into the wood frame and was dealt a sudden shock of guilt – as if she'd been scolded for touching it. Another time, a frustrated Harriet threatened it with a hammer and found herself standing out in the street, suddenly aware that hours had passed without memory. She did not threaten it again. She pondered moving it out of the bedroom, but feared what it might interpret her intentions to be – and how it might retaliate.

For her safety, she held cautious respect for the object, as she would a wild animal. It was dangerous and most likely deadly, but she decided – much like her present condition – it was best kept close and to herself.

She prepared for bed slowly, feeling the usual fatigue overtake her. Her joints ached right on cue, as if she might otherwise try to squeeze another hour out of the day if they didn't protest. She slipped into a gown and settled gradually onto the bed. To her benefit, the condition wiped her out nightly. As if the wine didn't provide enough incentive to relax, the fatigue settled her further, allowing her to fall quick and quiet into her final slumber.

It was a rest as deep and complete as she might have ever experienced. A freight train loaded to capacity with tornadoes could have rolled past her bed, and she'd have hardly stirred. To say death came peacefully was an understatement, but it came all the same.

The funeral director and his attendants acted with decorum, moving with haste and efficiency. They did not gossip, nor were they given to distraction. Who knows what might have happened had they taken a moment for themselves. Certainly, they would have forgotten poor Harriet completely with one half-hearted glance in the direction of the antique mirror.

Where once her reflection had been tucked gently into bed, mimicking her own prone form, it was now sitting bolt upright and staring, its face contorted in a mixed measure of surprise and anger. Its eyes burned; its mouth stretched as if open in a scream, but its lips never parted. Fingers tugged at the bedsheets impotently, daring anyone to notice it; no one did. No one looked, so no one noticed that her reflection remained long after Harriet's body had been taken away.

ONE

Cate's head reeled and she wondered where she was. It was an awful feeling to wake up without any sort of bearing on the world around her. Part of her brain knew that the pieces would click back together in a few moments as uniformity returned. That part was still dozing, leaving her scrambling for purchase. She was out of time and place, desperate for a crumb of knowledge to cling to. She rubbed her eyes and blinked hard. Blurry shapes swam around her, making a soft-edged puzzle of her surroundings. Fuzzy forms sharpened in contrast a little at a time as she strained to make sense of them.

A coffee table. A couch. Suddenly, a whole living room clicked into place. All at once, it came back to her. She exhaled in a rush, unaware that she'd been holding her breath.

I'm home…

It was bittersweet knowledge, waking at her parents' house. Recent memories lined up and took turns announcing themselves to her.

There was a phone call…

It took all of Cate's limited linguistic skills to decode her mother's garbled words. Hardly a language at all, it was more a mumbling whine, punctuated with howls and sobs. Even in the confusion, Cate felt blanketed by a strange, unnamed sadness. The sound of her mother's pain was so foreign to her that it created its own panic and fear.

"Mom?" She squeezed the phone in her grip, trying to strong-arm an answer from the other end of the call, but there was only more anguish arranged in a variety of new keys. In the end, it was a single word that communicated everything.

"…Harriet…" Even through her mother's miserable tears, the name intoned respect, love, and so many distressing questions.

The mere mention of her grandmother's name was all it took for Cate to drive through the night; she wanted to be there – *home* – as soon as she could. She hadn't bothered to pack, nor give a moment's consideration to sleep before the long drive. Even the luxury of a mid-journey motel room was beyond her. Instead, immediacy urged her on, eight hours straight through in the middle of the night.

It was long past the point of being able to turn around before she realized she told no one she was leaving. She remedied this with hurried, middle-of-the-night messages for both her boss and boyfriend. She knew Lucas would panic when he arrived home to find her missing. Everyone else would wait to worry when she didn't show up for work – or anywhere else – the next few days. The calls were clipped and to the point; her mind was all but fully occupied by her mother and grandmother.

Sound drifted to Cate in layers. The steady, filtered introduction of one sound after another compiled into an orchestra of morning life. She became aware of the sounds of someone going about their morning as delicately as possible: whispers, and careful, precise motions to reduce clatter. She smiled as she listened to her father, coaching himself through his work quietly, so he didn't disturb the slumbering vagabond on his couch.

It was a pleasant cacophony; one she was not used to. Cate always seemed to wake before Lucas, even when she slept in. The first sounds she heard in the morning were those of the city around her. That was a different soundscape than the one she found herself in presently. These sounds harkened back to her youth and made her smile.

Cate rubbed her eyes with the heels of her hands, hoping that enough friction might alleviate the burning in her sockets caused by too few hours' sleep on an uncomfortable couch. She picked up the half-full glass on the coffee table and took a long swallow. The room temperature tap water was barely enough to restore the desert that settled in her mouth while she slept. Unfortunately, it was also enough to rehydrate the film that had also accumulated there.

Uttering her disgust, she got to her feet, stumbling to the kitchen, her childhood memory guiding her through the floorplan. She sought water, but more so, she needed caffeine and aspirin. These were not serious issues, but Cate would happily ignore the misery that lingered in her heart for as long as she could.

Harriet was gone and suddenly nothing was right in the world. Even though she saw herself as strong and independent, it was moments like these that made her desperate for her parents to cradle her, hold her tight, and tell her it would all be okay – even if they had to lie. She wanted to hear it and believe it.

Surprisingly, her tears were light and infrequent as she left the city. It wasn't until she was alone with her thoughts on the desolate highway that they started to plague her. All of the memories of long car trips to grandma's house; of regular visits to grandma's favorite places: tea houses, yarn shops, and craft stores. She tried hard to ignore them, but they kept coming. Cate focused through the tears, keeping the wheels between blurring lines, her destination firmly in mind.

By some miracle, she made the trip without incident. It was surprisingly easy compared to the idea of actually doing it. Cate had only ever driven so far for so long in a single trip one other time. That was the day she moved away from small-town living to start a new life in a big, brand-new world.

She expected that life to be more about starting over and spreading her wings in a brand-new existence. Instead, it became a slow burn where she rekindled the same old life in a new place and new job. It frustrated her, but she limped along with good people. Better still, she found herself entwined in a storybook romance with a wonderful boy who wanted her as much as she wanted him, and it was everything to be wanted.

It wasn't until she saw the oh-so-familiar highway exit that she felt her stomach twist painfully. All the old town memories came back to her: How she *hated* this town growing up. It held nothing for her: blue-collar jobs, small bars, and an abundance of nothing for teens with the boundless energy of youth. It was the chief reason for the city's rampant drug issue, and further limited her options for quality people and interactions.

Cate considered intellect to be her favorite of man's abilities – that is, common sense and the sensibilities attached to it. She decided no one would ever tie her to a place that held her back or dumbed her down. No amount of begging, pleading, or bribery would shackle her to this dying town, not when there was something better out there – whatever and wherever it was.

Her escape plan hinged on finding a school that would accept her primarily on loans, while she desperately applied for every grant she even remotely qualified for. With tuition paid for, she added enough extra to sustain herself until she found a job. Then it was the mere matter of getting herself and her ugly little Subaru out of Dodge.

Cate pushed her way through school studying library sciences, nose comfortably tucked into one book after another. The thought of trapping herself in a room full of books for the next twenty or thirty years would be a fantastic way to spend a life. They could even bury her there when she was done, her own personal tomb. She wouldn't mind one bit.

As it turned out, libraries had the sort of turnover that she expected – no one quit being a librarian. It was a passion position. Why would anyone quit their dream job? So, the call hadn't come yet for the position of a lifetime. Cate was still waiting on it, still hoping for it.

In the meantime, she stumbled onto the next best thing. Wandering the downtown shops, Cate found a small bookstore. It was a cute little place that connected to the coffee shop next door. The bookstore had its own private order window, looking in on the baristas. It was the sort of shop that sold bestsellers, used books, independent authors, and handmade tchotchkes. You could hear slam poets working out their frustrations one night, then a children's author entertaining her young fans the next morning.

It was precisely the kind of shop Cate couldn't stop herself from falling in love with.

It was also where she met Lucas, the smiling boy with the shaggy blond hair and glasses that seemed too big for his face. Already in his mid-twenties, it seemed like a hope and a dare that he would grow into them. Cate found it to be a dorky kind of charm nonetheless. She was a day into learning the register when she knew beyond a doubt that she was in love with him.

She didn't say it, obviously; she wasn't insane. Only a lunatic tells a stranger those three magical words within the first twenty-four hours. She wouldn't say them in the first month, maybe not before the first year, if she wanted to play things safe. It was hard to keep it to herself, but somehow, she managed. Slowly though, clinging to her rationale, she fell deeper and harder for him. Charmed by his wit and demeanor, his love of "chick lit," and a passion for 14th and 15th century English poetry. It *almost* sounded like a line he used to pick up college girls, but when he actually discussed it, there was no mistaking his sincerity. Strange as it was to anyone else, he was genuinely into pre-Renaissance England. Cate could only assume that no one would fake such an interest. Perhaps it was her interest in him that made his fascinations palatable, she couldn't say, but becoming one of his interests definitely made his other hobbies even more worthwhile.

Time wore on between them: time together expanding and the distance between them contracting. She couldn't believe that she was actually talking to a boy this smart, soft-spoken, passionate, and interested in *her*.

It didn't take long for their relationship to begin climbing pedestals. First, it was the awkward, too-casual dates. This was after several hints that he should ask her out. She waited for his reserved demeanor to finally muster the courage to do so. Cate would bite her lip and tousle her hair in anticipation – apparently, that was too much. Lucas would disappear into the stockroom to find something more important to be doing around the store than chatting with her. He never stayed away too long, though. Maybe it was blind optimism, but Cate felt like his rebound was shorter with each interaction. She was mostly sure that he wanted to be there as much as she wanted him to be. Which meant they were destined to be together, right? They *had* to be together. Cate wasn't ready to consider a life where they weren't. Being around him was so magical that she needed it to be real.

New town, new job, new boy; her first *real* boy, she realized.

Of course, there were a couple of boys - what was high school without regrets? It was awkward and as terrible as it was terrific, but even then, Cate understood there was something better over the horizon. It was that flood of memories that crawled back to the front of her mind as she drove down the pre-dawn streets, fresh from her adventures beyond the horizon.

She found her way to her parents' house without GPS. Cate drove this route so many times, she could have gotten there by intuition alone. Her parents lived in the same place for most of her life, moving into the house when she was a toddler. When she moved out, they reclaimed her room, but promised her space whenever she needed it. She rarely accepted the invitation, not wanting to intrude. The offers continued, even after her parents retired and the house was regularly abandoned for weeks while they traveled. Invading their space when they were around was one thing, but the empty house felt less like intrusion and more like burglary.

She was certain that such intrusions must have felt similar to this. She crept into the house using the spare key hidden in the garden, kicking off her boots inside the door. She didn't even bother to take off her jacket as she shuffled into the living room and collapsed on the couch. She considered grabbing the blanket from her father's chair, but the rest of her brain decided that going to sleep immediately was a better, more manageable plan.

Groggily, she reintroduced herself to the world. Sleep had come, heavy, and refusing to be ignored. It wasn't until the first rays of morning found her shuttered eyelids, beaming to her from a slit in the blinds, did she become aware of morning as it existed around her unconscious form. Ahead of that introduction, she decided to air out the damp cocoon of her leather jacket from the night's passing. The seemingly simple task of shedding aged leather was first challenged by her half-awake and wholly uncaffeinated mind, further complicated by her tacky skin tugging against the jacket's lining. Her mouth tightened and she growled softly, her pace slowing as she tried to extricate herself from her captor and simultaneously walk a straight line to the kitchen - one complicated task too many for so early in the day.

"It lives! And it struggles. Here." Her father had come around the corner and was face-to-face with his adult daughter, struggling like an amateur escape artist and failing spectacularly. He managed to look startled without spilling his coffee. His face melted from surprise to whimsy as he helped her out of the twisted sleeves that bound her. "Seems like only yesterday we went through a similar row with your disastrous fashion sense."

"Dad, I was twelve," Cate paused, reflecting on the incident. "You were right about that shirt being too tight."

"Of course, I was. Would you like help tying your shoes next?"

"Ha ha, no. But you can pour me a cup of coffee."

"Already done." He leaned forward, pressing the warm mug into her hands. "Welcome home, sweetheart."

She put her arms around him, pressing her cheek into his shoulder. Part of her wished she would have dragged Lucas along for this, but she had insisted on this being something she needed to do herself. Stupid bravado. Her father's strong arms held her; he kissed her on the top of her head and she faltered. The happy moment short-lived as the rest of reality crashed in on her, reminding her why she was rousing in her parents' house.

"I can't believe she's gone." It rushed out of her mouth, pushed by a sudden flurry of tears. She felt him hold her tighter, one hand caressing her hair.

"I know, but she's in a better place now." The silence lingered, then he spoke again. "She's probably bossing around St. Peter already."

A small laugh got through the sadness, breaking up the tears momentarily and staunching the flow. She squeezed him tight and then let him go. He always knew the right thing to say to fix her.

Two

After a hearty breakfast, a couple of cups of coffee, and a hot shower, Cate returned to the living room. Her mother was still out; she had taken point on handling Harriet's affairs, which meant early mornings and long days to make sure that everything was squared away properly. No one wanted any want ugly surprises popping up later.

"She hasn't stopped long enough to let herself grieve yet," her father confided. "She's running the estate like she's back at the management company."

"Mom always liked being in charge."

"Still..." He hesitated, putting his cup of coffee down. "Can you talk to her? Maybe get her to relax a little. I'm afraid she's going to drive herself to her own heart attack."

Cate swallowed hard, suddenly aware of the next

pained beat of her own heart. "Is that what happened?"

He nodded, then wavered. "Sort of. Your grandmother had a condition."

"Since when?" This was news to Cate; Harriet wasn't one to keep secrets from her.

"We don't know. She kept it from *everyone*."

Harriet insisted that Cate always be honest with her, and promised the same in return. Why had she suddenly changed her mind?

"That's not Grandma." Cate shivered. Why would Harriet not tell her?

"I know. Her doctor said she didn't want anyone to stress over it."

"But she could have –" Her hands made half-hearted attempts to pluck at the air as she struggled with the proper words.

"That was exactly what she didn't want." He crossed the living room, sitting down on the couch beside her. He tried to smile as he put his arm around Cate.

"You know your grandma as well as I do – better, probably. She was selfless to the core. Remember when she almost lost her house?"

Cate nodded. "She couldn't make the house payment because she gave her money to all those charities."

"And the time she almost didn't make it to Christmas dinner?"

She laughed. "She loaned her car to one of the

neighbors so they could finish Christmas shopping."

He nodded, giving her another squeeze. "Does it surprise you that she might not say she was running out of time?"

"But I would have made so much more time for her if I'd only known." She punched her thighs for emphasis.

"She would have thought you were putting your life on hold to coddle a poor old woman." He patted her back gently.

She hugged him again, hiding in her father's arms, but the tears found her anyway.

"She was *my* poor old woman to coddle."

He said nothing. The waves of grief washed over her as he held tight. Caressing gently, the tremors eased and slowly, Cate found her way back toward peace. In the absence of turmoil, exhaustion overwhelmed her, calm filling in the vacuum. Gently, her father shifted Cate into the corner of the couch, covering her with a blanket and tucking it up to her chin as sleep caught up to her once again.

* * * *

Her father was right: her mother hadn't slowed down in the least. She had come home, bursting into the living room like a storm all her own. Cate was thrown from rejuvenating slumber back into the gale-force that was mom. This meant that she definitely hadn't given herself time to grieve. It was part of regular maintenance: purge the bad when it overwhelmed the system. When the bad was out, the good could return. Her mother was apparently not privy to this pro-tip and was certainly not listening to any other suggestions she'd been given so far. Her mother was never one for taking things slow – or at any pace other than full-speed. "Cate, hon, we are thinking about a memorial garden. A place where people can come and –"

"Really?" She stared over yet another cup of coffee. She'd lost count how many this was now. There was only the exhaustion and the coffee that kept it at bay. Was there such a thing as car lag? If there was, she must certainly have it.

"I'm sorry?" Her mother was staring. Maybe Cate spat the word out harsher than necessary.

"A memorial garden?" Her grandmother was a good person, a giving soul. She also preferred her modest life. She had nice things, but didn't go in for anything more than was necessary. "Was Grandma some secret heiress? How are you going to pay for something like that? Besides, no one is going to visit a garden dedicated to her."

"Well, the rest of the family –" Her mother began, but Cate was done listening.

"The rest of the family isn't going to visit either, except maybe on holidays when your garden is covered in a foot of snow."

Her mother stared; lips pursed tightly for a long minute. "If you don't like the idea, I'll drop it."

"Mom, I like the idea of a garden. But for you."

"I don't need a garden."

"Neither does she. She's gone."

Her mother stared at her, eyes glittering as if some unspoken rule had been broken. The thin, angry line of her mouth quivered as if it hadn't decided whether it wanted to be angry or sad. Before any more words could be said out of turn, Cate wrapped her arms around her mother and pulled her close, sputtering with tears that had been building up inside.

"She wouldn't want you ignoring your feelings, either. She'd want you to get the sad part out of the way so you can laugh during the wake."

There was a huff of laughter, a shuddering breath, then a broken heaving wail. Cate held tight as her mother buckled; the sadness that had been shoved down and ignored poured out in a deluge. Cate helped her to a chair, staying close. She pulled the box of tissues close and dragged a couple out for when the storm subsided.

Minutes passed as she sat with her mother, wanting to ease the pain and feeling utterly helpless to do anything. Slowly, the sobbing ebbed. Her breath less ragged with each intake, but still shaky as she tried to exhale without breaking down into another fit of tears. Finally came the deep exhale of relief that signaled the end of the seemingly infinite sadness.

Her mother dabbed at her eyes, giving a sheepish smile to Cate.

"I must look like hell now."

Cate smiled back. "It's fine. You're allowed."

"Thank you."

The moment between them was a quiet one. A warm moment, lacking the usual awkwardness that filled the silences between mother and daughter. Cate reached out and dragged her mother's overstuffed handbag over to her side of the table, pulling out a notebook bursting with opened envelopes, tri-folded pages, and sticky notes marking essential passages. The amount of additional material transformed the simple journal into a bloated binder. The sheer sight of it intimidated Cate, but she also knew with that first good cry out of the way, it was the perfect time to start chipping away at the responsibilities.

"Now, let's see if I can help with any of this."

THREE

The tumblers turned, the deadbolt sliding out of the way with a final click. Cate felt like they were opening a long-abandoned sarcophagus. It was honestly worse than invading her parents' home when they weren't around. This was breaking in *and* sneaking around. She had to remind herself that there was no sneaking around if no one was ever coming back. The thought did not comfort her as much as she thought it should.

The funeral, the wake, and most of the tears were over with. All that remained now was to take care of the leftovers, which Cate insisted she help with. Her mother tried to refuse the offer, but Cate stuck close, knowing her mother was running on empty.

After a couple of misdialed numbers, Cate's mother

threw her hands up in frustration, the phone flipping end over end before thudding to a halt on the carpet. Her frustration, compounded by her exhaustion, did nothing to ease the stress of burying a parent, nor the anxiety of having to prep a house for market. Cate comforted her as best she could, one mourner to another, and then guided her mother to Harriet's recliner, if only to relax for a moment. In the time it took for Cate to return from the kitchen with a glass of water, her mother was fast asleep. With a silent cheer of triumph, Cate recovered the cellphone from its all-but-forgotten place on the floor.

Moving back to the kitchen, she began working her way down the list of creditors and utilities. More than one argument ensued, Cate finding that she was quite good at communicating dissatisfaction by tone, even without volume. She wasn't sure what she'd done to get the worst of the operators at each of these establishments, but with each call, she was closer to earning her heavenly reward. She closed credit lines, cut ties with the cable man, and scheduled shut-offs for gas, electric, and water. Cate had an oddly pleasant conversation with the credit card company and the bank; both parties wanting to ensure that accounts were handled correctly and the proper paperwork was collected on both sides.

After calling around to get details taken care of, and informing the realtor that they would have a place for him to show very soon, Cate turned her attention to the last awful detail: cleaning house.

Cate stood in the kitchen, where she waited for some dramatic realization. It dawned on her that nothing appeared to be out of place. The dishes were all in their rightful locations; each throw pillow sat in its prescribed nook. She wandered down the hall, looking for some indicator that this awful thing had happened; that a great light had been snuffed out within these walls. Instead, she looked around and found everything in its proper place. Nothing was amiss at all. It was like Harriet stepped out, and she'd be back any minute.

The notion made everything better and worse at the same time. Better because Grandma Harriet was a meticulous organizer. Everything would have a place and no item would be very far from where it belonged. What made things worse was that she and her mother were responsible for cataloging everything in the house. That meant wading through memories – and tears – both happy and sad, to get to the end of this project.

After Cate's tour of procrastination and her mother's nap, they started in the kitchen, agreeing that it was probably the least emotionally volatile room in the house. Cate decided that too much emphasis had been implied on the sad end of the scale and that the phrase "emotionally volatile" needed to be revisited. Tears were a response that could be applied to many emotions; frustration was another emotion that could generate tears – specifically produced by withholding the irritation brought on by her mother's childlike barrage of questions.

"Do you need any spatulas?"

"No, they can go in the box."

"What about whisks?"

"In the box."

"How about a mixer?"

"I don't bake, Mom."

"You might if you had a mixer."

"No, I never got one because I don't bake."

"Maybe you should try it. You might impress Louis."

"Lucas."

"What happened to Louis?"

"There's never been a Louis."

"Are you sure?"

"Mom, do you think I don't know who I am dating?"

"Well, if you can't remember what happened to Louis…"

They went back to their respective duties. Cate wrapped and packed glassware while her mother organized the utensils. Cate continued to handle the obvious items that would be boxed and either sold or donated, while her mother sorted through things someone – though she usually meant Cate – in the family might be able to use.

"What about recipe books?"

"Grandma didn't really cook, she baked. I don't."

"But they're books."

"About baking, Mom."

"I didn't know you segregated. I thought you loved *all* books."

She stopped what she was doing and took the time to actually turn and shake her fist at her mother. It angered her even more that her mother reduced her to something so cliché. Her frustration was at such a boiling point that she almost missed her mom trying to suppress a laugh.

"I'm sorry; I had to!" She held up her hands, surrendering to both Cate and her own laughter. Cate, in reply, wadded up the newspaper in her hand and threw it in an ugly curve that missed in a wide arc.

"That's not funny." Cate tried to conceal her own smile, but she was infected.

Her mother continued to chuckle. "Your face... I wish I had taken a picture."

"You're a little too pleased with yourself."

"Wait till your father hears."

"Oh, god."

FOUR

They managed to clear the rest of the kitchen and the living room without incident. Cate moved into the guest room, which doubled as Harriet's sewing room. It was the most straightforward task she could have been put on.

As the room was still occasionally used for guests, all of the sewing materials were stored in bins and organized. Thread was organized by weight, use, and color. Needles and machine parts were found in a caddy, each component in its own tray. Fabrics were rolled up on themselves and collected in innumerable bins, stacked one upon the next in the corner of the room. It amazed her that one person could collect so much fabric – and proceed to not use it. Thread, too, in every color of the rainbow and multiple spools of each were collected in large plastic containers, all arranged and organized like some sort of giant seamstress' tackle box.

Cate didn't have to go through the craft supplies; it was all moving on. Whether that meant that one of her aunts or cousins might take the antique sewing machine on its own, or if they'd take the fabrics and thread as well, remained to be seen. But she knew that nothing was going to her parents' house and it definitely wasn't going home with her – her mother knew better than to even ask.

The amount of fabric and related paraphernalia continued to baffle her, but Cate supposed that someone could say the same about her book collection. *Why would anyone need so many books,* they might ask, and she would smile and shrug and politely scrub the person from her life. It was pointless to discuss such topics with anyone who would bother asking such questions. These were people who didn't understand collecting; they didn't enjoy possessions. Maybe they didn't understand books, heaven forbid. They were people who couldn't sit still, who moved when they got bored, moving with the end of each lease, time and again. They uprooted themselves, but never relocated; they never left for some new and unfamiliar locale. They were comfortable moving from one plot of land to another in the same dying field, townies from cradle to grave. They didn't understand Cate, and Cate didn't understand them. It was an impasse and she was more than comfortable never returning to the subject if she could at all help it.

She stacked the boxes in the closet but left the doors open. She didn't trust movers. In her own experiences, they were largely unobservant. They usually missed something and left Cate to move a bunch of boxes herself. She didn't want anything left behind and she didn't want to lug any of the boxes herself when they had a company to do it for them.

Yet there was a feeling – a cocktail of paranoia and unnamable suspicion – nagged at her, insisting she should move everything out into the living room so there would be no confusion. She pushed back against the persistent notion; it seemed like a lot of lifting and heaving and she had already exhausted her sick time on this trip. She would just have to trust these movers to their duty. She didn't have time to recover comfortably if she pulled a muscle.

It wasn't that she regretted making the trip. It was necessary, but it was a point of frustration for her. It was aggravating that company policy didn't include grandparents in bereavement – immediate family only: parents, spouses, siblings, and children. She'd have to inform Lucas he wasn't allowed to die unless they either got married or broke up… and she wasn't wasting sick days on an ex-boyfriend.

She broke out of her reverie, moving down the hall to the master bedroom. It appeared that her mother was a whirlwind of organization when no one was in the way.

The dresser and the closets were already empty, a stack of boxes amassed along one bare wall. The bed had been stripped of its finery and was now adorned with a gallery's worth of picture frames. Cate moved to the bed to look at them. Each frame was matted and sectioned with multiple pictures laid out within: Harriet's parents, her childhood, her wedding; plenty of pictures of Grandpa Jake and the family they had together all the way down to the grandchildren, Cate included

Family photos seemed like a great lost art to Cate. None of her friends had these sprawling histories hanging from their walls; no one seemed to anymore – definitely no one under the age of forty. It wasn't that people stopped taking pictures. Far from it, they took plenty; Cate was no exception. The trouble was that they were all collected on her phone, or on social media, and not a single one of those photos was the overwhelming production of getting the whole family dressed up for a reunion photo or commemorating the milestone memory of Aunt Steph's baptism. Things didn't seem to have the same grand scale in Cate's life that they had in Harriet's.

Her photos could be broken up into three categories: The first being photographic documentation from the world of culinary delights – mostly eating, not so much making. The second gallery contained numerous seemingly same pictures of Lucas, with and without Cate; several hundred pictures of Sebastian, her spoiled Maine Coon, with and without Cate. On a rare occasion, she could get a good photo with her two favorite men together. Lastly, there were selfies. So many selfies. Admittedly, much like her photos of Lucas and Sebastian, they hardly differed from one another. Some were precious and tied to some beloved memory, but as many as there were, when they were displayed one after another, they looked eerily similar. Sometimes her hair was up, sometimes she had makeup on, but it was always the same angle, the same smile, and the same fragment of obliterated background that could hardly differentiate itself from any other selfie.

Her thoughts were interrupted by movement caught in her periphery. She looked up and, for a moment, her brain didn't quite register what she was seeing. Part of her expected it to be her mother – a small hopeful part wanted it to be her grandmother – but in the end, it was only Cate.

She stared at herself, dark circles staring back. She frowned, her hair looking as limp as her posture. It was clear by the way she shuffled listlessly around the bed, Cate was weary. Her brow wrinkled as her eyes scrutinized the corner of the room. She hadn't noticed the mirror at all when she walked in, like it had been hiding and then emerged from its hiding place while she had been turned.

Cate massaged the bridge of her nose. She could feel exhaustion squeezing in on her brain. She hadn't seen the mirror because she had walked into the room in a fugue. The motion out of the corner of her eye had alerted her, drawing her attention to the accent piece occupying the corner. That was all, nothing crazy, just exhaustion and inattention.

The looking glass was extravagant. It wasn't so much a mirror as it was a doorway. The glass itself was so immaculate Cate almost believed she could walk right through into a matching mirror room.

The large frame rested on a sturdy base. It was considerably taller than her, possibly even taller than the doorway, staring down at her with its deep chestnut wood. Carved feet stuck out from both front and back. Not that she thought it needed anything to support it, the wood frame itself was wider than her palm, inches thick, and could easily provide an ample base area to keep the monolith standing. Cate assumed they were more of a precaution to keep sweet old ladies from being crushed under its impressive weight, should it topple over. For a moment, the sadness of her grandmother's passing threatened to creep in again, but the caricature of her grandmother's fuzzy purple slippers sticking out from beneath the wooden giant evaporated the tears and provided her a small, impish smile. She could hardly imagine the number of years invested in its construction by some nameless master woodworker. Cate poked around it, examining the wood up close, unable to see any traces of seams or joints. It was as if the mirror's housing had been carved from a single piece of wood, rather than milled and puzzled together. It was a masterclass in artisanal craftsmanship – none of that so-called artisanal junk from the farmers' market. This was the real deal.

She shook her head, the cobwebs thick as they shook loose from her thoughts. There was no way that her grandmother was sitting on a one-of-a-kind, giant, hand-carved mirror and never worked it into a conversation. Not once had Harriet ever pointed it out when Cate visited. Her mother would have been sure to say something, maybe even send a picture or two.

Her thoughts lingered on the mystery of this mirror, but her eyes drifted back to the detail around the frame. The wood was accented with deep looping grooves that wandered down the length of the frame along the sides of the glass. The grooves chased one another around the corners, knotting and entwining before they emerged in a similar ambling loop that scored its way across the bottom of the frame.

At the top, the frame arched and at its apex hung dried flowers. She stepped closer, squinting harder. They weren't dried, but wooden carvings. A bouquet of wooden cherry blossoms hung from the medallion centerpiece at the top of the mirror. She gaped at how realistic the flowers appeared to be. Petals curled in their own directions, each one as thin and fragile as the genuine article.

She stared as she moved in a semicircle around the front of the mirror, entranced by the flowers. Something was bothering her about the arrangement, something more than the discovery of wood carvings so intricate. Cate felt like she was descending into the uncanny valley but couldn't pinpoint what was dragging her there. Craning her neck up at the centerpiece was giving her a kink. She pulled her phone out of her pocket and snapped some pictures of the carving, zooming in as she rested up against the bed. She magnified the image, examining as closely as her height, her camera, and the zoom function would allow. Still, she couldn't see the secret begging to be discovered. She flipped back and forth, frustrated with her inability to puzzle it out.

The longer she thought about it, the more infuriated and impatient she became. She flipped the pictures back and forth faster and faster in the gallery until they were motion blur to her eyes. She slapped her thumb down on the screen. Her jaw was tight as she looked down, ready to lift her thumb and start deleting pictures. Suddenly, there it was. Raising her phone, she looked at the photos on display. Her thumb had paused between photos, a thin frame separating one from the other. The thin section of picture that was not yet off-screen seemed to reflect the other image. She dragged her thumb across the screen, examining the two photos and their eerie similarities.

She looked up at the carving again with a new perspective. The bas-relief appeared to be perfectly symmetrical. The looping grooves revealed themselves to be inverted vines that wound down the mirror's frame. It didn't seem possible to exist with the amount of detail it appeared to have. Yes, it explained the uncanny valley vertigo she felt, but it raised more questions than it answered. It couldn't have been carved by hand, could it? No human being of any age or mastery could carve with such exacting detail – not without machinery, and then it couldn't have been hand-carved… maybe it hadn't been carved after all.

Still, there it was. A bizarre bouquet that seemed to have died on the vine as it bathed under some forgotten sun. She stepped closer again, now noticing the vague imprint of leaves in the flat expanses of wood, as if they'd been pressed, leaving an impression.

Cate had never seen anything like it, even in the traditional drawings and carvings she'd seen on visits to museums. It unsettled her. What about the mirror that made her skin crawl so?

Her question was swallowed up in stunned silence as she stared at the glass. Though the frame itself – new as it appeared – dated itself to a time long ago, the glass looked brand new. It shimmered like silver, yet it was practically translucent. Without reaching out and touching the glass, Cate couldn't be sure it was there at all. She stared for a minute at herself, feeling like she was standing in front of her doppelgänger. The other Cate watched and waited, making precise pantomime opposite her own motions. The longer she stared at the reflection, and the clarity with which she saw herself, the more Cate wondered which side of the mirror she was actually on.

She held up a hand, waving it slowly back and forth in front of her. The other Cate complied, copying her flawlessly. She continued to wave, first the right hand, then the left, back and forth. As she waved, she felt herself take small steps closer to the mirror. Something compelled her to close the distance between herself and the reflection until there was barely a breath between herself and her reflection. Even there, with no distance between herself and the glass, it seemed unbelievable that there could be any sort of reflective surface separating them. Again, she felt a tug to move closer, as if she could reach out and–

"I told you that you were pretty too often."

The jolt that surged through her body started in her feet and ended in her head as she banged her nose against the mirror. Reeling back to gain balance and whatever composure she could muster, she turned to stare at her mother. Holding her nose and struggling for some kind of reply, the silence slowly filled with awkwardness as she stared, part angry, part embarrassed, all frazzled. Her mother smiled, gesturing to the boxes in the closet beside her.

"Would you be a dear and help me carry these boxes out to the living room?"

Presuming no lasting damage from the incident, Cate

took the first box from her mother, expelling a huff of breath as the deceptively heavy container threatened to take her to the floor as it made an attempt at escape. She waddled a bit before adjusting her grip on the box so she could comfortably walk all the way out to the living room, her mother following directly behind her with another – undoubtedly lighter – container.

"All of this can go directly to the trash when we get out of here - unless you can find a use for any of your grandmother's toiletries."

The mere mention of used toiletries made Cate shudder a little. The phrase carried the same weight for her that 'moist' did for others. But the idea of using any of her grandmother's bathroom leftovers, well, that was worse in so many more ways.

"Um, no. I'm fine, thanks. When did grandma get the old mirror?"

"That enormous thing in the bedroom? She's had that for years." She paused a moment, Cate feeling the air thicken with the threat of sadness again. "I think she got it after dad – *my* dad – passed away."

The moment hung; her mother swallowed hard and nodded her head vigorously. "I'm almost certain."

"Really? Why don't I remember it?"

"She wouldn't let anyone near it." She shrugged, but a new thought crept into mind. "She seemed so proud of it at first. But then, she wouldn't let near her bedroom. The door was always closed; she said she didn't want anyone to damage it." Her mom hesitated, her mouth twisting with concentration. "I don't think that was really the reason."

Cate paused, huffing again as she put the box down. "What do you think the real reason was?"

Her mother shook her head, running a hand through her hair before shrugging.

"I don't know. Clearly, she had her secrets. She was always peculiar about it, though."

Cate took a couple of steps backward, twisting to look back down the hallway again.

"What if it's drugs?"

"What?"

Cate's eyes widened. "Yeah, what if she was dealing drugs and they were hidden in the mirror?"

"Cate, really…"

She clapped her hands together. "No, wait. Grandma was way more likely to be hiding something else. Maybe she was a serial killer and that's where she hid her keepsakes?"

Her mother was flabbergasted. "That's not funny."

Cate pointed a severe finger at her mother. "You're right; it's not. Innocent blood was likely shed all over that mirror in the name of her dark lord!"

"Cate!" Her mother called, but it was too late. Cate was already down the hall and back to the bedroom, her fingers roaming the edges of the mirror and she leaned around the frame, looking for some sort of secret hidey-hole in the wood.

"Catherine Irene! Stop right now!"

Cate froze, her inner child petrified at the incantation that had risen from her mother's throat. Those words, in the right tone, were communication all their own. It was a threat that communicated two things: First, that she had gone too far; second, that if she persisted, she would hear the full incantation: all three names. It was a severe warning at any age – three names was a doorway to punishment. Even as a grown adult, Cate's spine sang with nervous energy. She backed delicately away from the mirror, using small, slow movements. It was the same slow-motion pantomime she imagined using if she were ever in serious trouble with the police.

Turning, she made eye contact with her mother, arms taut and akimbo, her lips in a stern line. Her mother's arms were crossed, sinews taut as they pulled against tense forearms. But what Cate focused on was the speckling of tears brimming in her mother's eyes. "You take things too far sometimes."

"Sorry."

Cate had a sinking feeling that her mother was more like Grandma Harriet than she wanted to be. Whether she knew the reason or not, she was quick to whip up a tornado around the old mirror and the "don't look, don't touch" policy. Cate relaxed, moving to her mother's side as they stared down the hall together, considering the monstrosity.

"So, what are we going to do with it?" The question hung in the air for a long minute. Cate didn't want to suggest anything – she had no idea how attached her mother was to the object – but she had to start somewhere. "It might sell for a good price to a collector."

"Yeah, maybe." Her mother shrugged, her mouth dancing back and forth in debate. The words lingered as if the thought was unfinished.

"Maybe?" Cate poked, trying to jostle the thought loose from her mother's brain.

Slowly, her mother's gaze turned away from the hall, her stance easing from its rigidity as she leaned into Cate. Cate felt a cold chill as her mother smiled.

"…or, we could find a way to secure it to your car before you head home."

FIVE

"You've got a what?"

Lucas's voice paused on the other end of the line. Cate wasn't sure if he hadn't heard her or if he couldn't will himself to believe her.

"A mirror. A *huge* mirror and it's strapped to my roof!" She tried to glare into the phone as he chuckled. "It's not funny! It's going to take me forever to get home because of this thing."

"Tie it down better."

"It's tied down fine. I'm afraid a good gust of wind is going to turn me into an airplane. I'm going to have to take back roads the whole way."

"How did you wind up with a giant mirror?"

Cate opened her mouth to explain, but a strangled

squeak was all she could muster. She didn't really know how. Her mother had offered it to her and she had intended to say no, but the word never sounded. Instead, she had said yes – literally the opposite of her intention. She couldn't explain why; it was a strange insistence that compelled her to do so. Cate tried to explain it all again in a second squeak. Lucas had not yet mastered Cate-lish, but he was trying.

Lucas suppressed a sigh, but she caught the initial release. She knew he was dealing with a lot right now: what started with her rushing away in the middle of the night to deal with a death in the family had inexplicably ended with her moving elephantine antiques back home. In trade for his bottomless patience, she had offered a couple of incomprehensible squeaks.

"I have to move a giant mirror when you get back, don't I?"

Her smile broke wide.

"Have I told you how much I love that big beautiful brain of yours?"

"Flattery will get you –"

"Everywhere?"

"...maybe. But there's going to have to be more flattery involved."

"I'm sure that can be arranged."

There was a laugh and their thoughts wandered in their own separate directions. She knew exactly which direction Lucas' mind was heading in, and she couldn't really blame him. At some point, she'd heard that funerals – or maybe it was deep remorse in general – brought lurid desires and improper thoughts to the surface. She hadn't had any inappropriate thoughts in the time she had been home, but she also hadn't made time for that kind of thinking. That, and Lucas was also at a terribly inconvenient distance should she need his assistance. Perhaps it was self-preservation that pushed him from her thoughts. She sighed and smiled gently, the tension easing out of her shoulders a little as the miles passed beneath her. There would be plenty of time to deal with her emotional overload when she was back in his arms.

"How big is this mirror?"

She tried to describe the mirror to him and found that she couldn't quite convey the description. It was evident that he got the gist and understood the enormity of the mirror itself. Still, she continued to describe it, trying to convey the emotional gravity she felt when she looked at the mirror. There was something special about it, but not something that could be easily described. He would have to see it for himself to truly understand.

"Are we going to need extra hands to get this thing upstairs?"

"Maybe? I mean, we can definitely do it. Dad and I got it out of the house and on top of the car."

"Ok, so when will you be back?"

"I'm already heading out of town. I think I am going to have to pull off somewhere tonight and finish the trip in the morning. Definitely won't be later than tomorrow night."

"Good."

"What?"

"I miss you."

Cate smiled, semi-consciously pushing harder on the accelerator. "I miss you too. I'll be home before you know it."

"I doubt that. Sebastian has been announcing every minute you've been gone. Around the clock."

She couldn't help but coo, more to herself than to Lucas. Sebastian had warmed up to Lucas since they moved in together, but the furball would always prefer her company to his. If she disappeared for longer than a workday, she returned to find him waiting by the door, cool-eyed judgment clear on his feline face. Then, with a flick of his tail, he would leave her to plead and explain herself before he would grant her the attention they both were looking for.

"Oh god, give him a big hug and tell him I'll be home tomorrow."

"I don't think he'll believe me, but I'll tell him."

They talked for a while longer, discussing the goings-on she missed at the bookstore, and what Lucas had been doing to keep occupied. Eventually, she sent him to bed, wishing him good night, and turned up the radio.

Cate put as many miles between her and her loss as she could in an exhausting evening. She drove until her eyes started to cross; her keen focus on the road melting into a blur of blacktop and yellow stripes.

Finding a rest area, she parked and skipped out to the facilities to freshen up before retiring to her cramped little room at Chez la Car. Cate rolled the seat back and covered up with her jacket. She rocked back and forth, willing the seatback to extend a couple inches wider, as she tried to find a position to fall asleep. Uncomfortable as she was, it wasn't long before sleep overtook her, exhaustion overriding the discomfort of her roadside retreat.

Six

She opened her eyes, feeling refreshed, and expected to see the sun casting light into the car's interior. In fact, she expected to see anything. It was still dark, both outside and inside the vehicle. Cate sat up, immediately regretting the decision. Her head swam with a sudden invisible thickness as she twisted in her seat, trying to get her bearings. She looked around in the dark, massaging her temples and wondering exactly how long she might have slept.

Maybe it was a power nap? It was hardly conclusive, but a possibility.

She adjusted the seatback to a locked and upright position. She relaxed her hands on the steering wheel and realized she was instinctively resetting to the driving position, as if ready to depart. She paused, shook her head, and reclined the seat two clicks. It wouldn't be wise to get on the road so quickly – not until she understood how awake she actually was. She didn't want to get on the road, only for exhaustion to take her when she was far from a safe place to rest. Trusting her fate to the great distance between herself and home and hoping for the best wasn't something she was inclined to try.

She slid the seat so she could extend her legs again, fiddling with her water bottle. In the dark, it was hard to tell which end of the symmetrical cylinder was the screw-top/cup combination, and which was aesthetic. Finally getting the bottle open, she took a long drink.

She winced; the water tasted tinny and old. It didn't taste like the water she had filled the bottle with before leaving. It was neither crisp nor refreshing; it tasted as if it had been waiting a long time to be released.

Cate wiped at her mouth and put the bottle in the cupholder. Her lips smacked, trying to rid themselves of the foul taste. She relaxed in the driver seat, trying to close her eyes and rest. After a handful of minutes, Cate decided that it probably wasn't exhaustion, nor had it been a power nap. Dawn was probably on the other side of the horizon, waiting for her to begin their shared journey. Nodding to herself that now was as good a time as any, she considered this turning into a windfall that made up some time while traffic was minimal. She turned the key in the ignition and flicked the headlights on. The engine cranked begrudgingly to life. Through the windshield, the world was still black.

She flicked the lights off and then back on. The dashboard reacted to the command, all of her instruments lighting up their little faces and symbols to inform her that all systems were ready to engage. Outside the windows, darkness continued to press in against the glass. The lights didn't fire, their absence implying that nothing seemed to exist beyond her windows in the inky blackness.

Cate reached for the window controls and hesitated. Part of her knew there was no reason to be afraid, that this must be dense fog, or faulty headlights or some other reasonable explanation. Another part of her insisted the window remain closed. That same fearful part of her insisted that something unnatural was on the other side of the windows and that it would be unwise to compromise the safety of the car she was contained in.

She obliged that screaming portion of her brain and stared into the dark, moving her hand away from the controls. There was nothing outside – absolutely nothing. The darkness was so complete that it was almost as if someone had painted her windows as a prank.

She tried to put that thought out of her imagination. If that was true, she was equally in trouble. What if they were still out there, waiting for her to exit the car? What if this was a kidnapping?

She shook it off. Cate knew she was being paranoid. How likely was it that they would target the beaten-up hatchback? One better: how hard could it be to abduct a sleeping woman from said hatchback? Especially one that could not afford a practical way to move an oversized mirror.

She grabbed her phone and clicked the flashlight button. She squinted for a moment as she angled the light so that it would shine out the window without blinding her. She peered, trying to see around her reflection. She moved to the left, then to the right, but her reflection was always smack in the middle of her and the pitch dark beyond.

Cate sighed deeply and leaned in, hoping to see through the reflection. Her own face obscured her vision to the point of frustration. She was ready to give up, an exercise in futility. But before she could move away from the window, her reflection leaned to the side.

Cate jumped back, dropping the phone. There was no way she could have seen that. She rubbed her eyes, starbursts of green and purple erupted over and again in the darkness while her eyes adjusted. She pawed along the floor, her fingers searching for the lip of the case that had slipped between the seat and the console. Light cast up and down along the molded plastic, exaggerated shadows danced around her grasping digits. Gasping in relief, she closed her fingers around the phone, the car erupting with light again as she drew the light up into the open again.

She pulled the phone up, shining it at the window and almost screamed. She wanted to, but it had caught in her throat, afraid to come out. Her reflection was leaning in, head cocked to the side and examining her like a predator seeing human prey for the first time. Quickly, she turned the light away, scrambling over the gearshift and armrest to get to the passenger side, far from the strange reflection. Once clear, she held the light up, squinting around the light shining back at her to see that there was nothing in or outside the driver's side window. Her breath came quick as her light darted up and down the car, her eyes following frantically. Minutes passed without further incident, allowing her to breathe deep and slow her racing pulse. It was clear that she was in no condition to drive if she was hallucinating.

Again, her mind cried out that this might not be a hallucination. Someone might be outside the car. Either way, the darkness was still a concern, still too complete. She shuffled around in her seat to look out the passenger side window. When she'd gone to sleep, she was in a parking spot, but nothing had been around her. Had she been walled in by bigger vehicles while she slept?

She lifted the flashlight again and her reflection was there, menacing her. Cate tried to resist, but whether her exhaustion or her frayed nerves has wrested control from her, the scream ripped through her vocal cords, filling the silence of the car and the night.

Her reflection did not scream with her. Instead, it continued to stare, heavy-browed and angry-eyed, leaning against the window to leer and intimidate in a way Cate could not imagine herself doing.

Cate's scream continued into consciousness, where she sat bolt upright in her driver seat.

SEVEN

Around her, traffic moved slowly through the rest stop, largely unaware of Cate's crisis. A couple paused, startled by the outburst. They didn't look long before moving onward to the vending machines, public bathrooms, and maps of local attractions. Beyond them, she could see the highway functioning normally, the morning sky evenly lighting all of the activity around her.

Cate looked from window to window. Nowhere in her field of vision was the inky black that had persisted moments before. Also absent was her sinister reflection, evaporated in the morning sky. She adjusted the seat back and leaned into it, breathing deep and slow, as her heartbeat edged back from its thunderous pace. One hesitant gesture at a time, Cate got out of the car, navigating the sidewalks to the bathroom. She tried to follow the pattern along the walk, keeping her feet under her and in a straight line; she could not keep herself from weaving, as if she left her equilibrium behind in the car.

At the sink, Cate let the water run cold, splashing her face over and over. She visualized the residual fear and confusion washing down the drain with the swirling water. Pulling at her t-shirt, she stretched it into a makeshift towel to dry her face.

As the fabric slipped down her face, she locked eyes with her reflection. Cate couldn't help but stare, afraid to move. A familiar girl stared back at her, brown eyes wild and afraid. Her hair was mess, sticking out in shoots, only adding to her feral look. Breaking contact with her reflection, she kept her head down, refusing to meet her own gaze again, or even look anywhere near the mirrored surface. She didn't want to see it change again. She let the damp shirt drop and exited the facility, bee-lining for her car again.

She slumped back into the car seat, gathering herself and reminding herself of the route home. She took a deep breath and started the car. Pulling carefully out of the spot, she crawled through the pedestrian pathways and moved toward the highway onramp. She checked her gauges, her side mirrors, and instinctively looked up to catch her own eye in the rearview mirror. She shuddered, meeting her own gaze, then reached up, tugging the mirror off its hanger and tossed it in the back seat. The last thing she wanted on her last leg home was an unnecessary distraction.

Eight

Lucas stared at the car as it pulled up to the curb of the apartment building. He shuffled in place; trading looks with best friend. Michael looked back at him, shoulders slumping. Whether the tell was subconscious, Lucas didn't know, but he was fully aware that the look in Michael's eyes said that he was calculating exactly how much the couple would owe for his services. Cate put the car in park hurriedly, excited to be out of the car, hardly concerned with the car's violent see-sawing as it settled in place.

She leapt the curb, putting her arms around the first of the perplexed men, squeezing Lucas tight. She boosted herself up on her tiptoes and kissed his cheek. He did not return the kiss, barely putting an arm around her as she pressed against him.

"I'm glad to see I was missed."

His eyes were still fixed on the top of the car, his mouth twitching reflexively.

"Where is it going to live?"

"How are we going to get it upstairs?" Michael interjected, trying not to sound as daunted as Lucas.

"It's fine, cowards. We can manage."

They both turned to her, stunned. Only Lucas could find the words to refute her confidence.

"Can we? It's enormous!"

She gave him another playful squeeze, smiling to herself as she caught the gentle scent she'd been missing. "I thought you had a solution for everything."

"Congratulations, you have found my one weakness."

"Family heirlooms?"

"Giant housewares."

She broke the embrace and wandered back to the car, unfastening the straps that held the mirror to the roof. Michael went to one side while Lucas went to the other. Cate moved to the back and, slowly, they worked the mirror down the hatch of the car and, step by step, guided it up the apartment stairs.

The apartment building was originally a row of large brownstone homes. Now, the refurbished rooms were sectioned off into individual living areas within the block of dwellings. It was where Cate and Lucas had already shared two years of blissful togetherness. Part of the attraction, beyond the timeless feel of the old neighborhood was the oversized doorways, the wide halls, and the imposing stone staircase that greeted tenants and passersby alike.

So many good weather days were spent greeting neighbors from the other side of a paperback novel as they both sprawled across the wide porch steps. Front porch cookouts bent the laws of physics, managing to seat practically everyone in the building without a single chair, yet able to keep the grill away from the public sidewalk where pedestrians might bring trouble. Even their apartment, a simple and small one-bedroom, seemed to bend the rules of space to provide them enough room for everything they owned and still somehow managed to be spacious enough for entertaining.

One step at a time, they managed to get the mirror into the building, up the winding staircase, and into the apartment. Together, they guided it smoothly into the bedroom, where it seemed the room itself had made a place for the mirror. The entire way, they were amazed that the mirror never seemed to be a struggle; it seemed to always be the perfect size to get through the next obstacle without issue.

"As if it were meant to be," Lucas poked at her again and again. Each time, she stuck her tongue out and reminded him that it was better easy, rather than struggling the whole way. Michael, who had initially thought he was in over his head, admitted he was pleasantly surprised by the lack of work he put forth in trade for a free meal.

As it happened, Sebastian became the only obstacle slowing progress. From the moment the door opened and he caught sight and sound of Cate, Sebastian was crazed for her attention. He circled like a frenzied shark, mewling until he was more of a hazard than her help was worth. She broke off from the heavy lifting to hold the frantic bowling ball of brown striped fluff desperate for her affection, leaving Lucas and Michael to navigate the apartment in peace.

"I know, I missed you too! I did!" He dug claws into her top, pulling her closer so he could nuzzle her face to face. She held him close, nuzzling and kissing him until he settled into her arms, purring loud enough for her to feel the vibration in her chest and arms. She stroked down his spine, feeling paws knead at the arm that was supporting him. Smiling, they followed the mirror into the bedroom. She wondered to herself who was carrying the heavier parcel. Neither Lucas nor Michael appeared to be struggling, while already, her elbow began to ache under the weight of her oversized not-tiger. Lucas and Michael stood the mirror up and slowly unraveled the wrapping that protected it on the long journey to its new home.

"Wow," Lucas stepped back, taking in the full view once the monstrosity was settled into place.

"See? It *is* like it belongs here." She curled Sebastian

into the crook of one arm, then curling into the crook of one of Lucas's. She pulled him close, feeling his arm slip around her waist, squeezing gently and finally providing the much-needed attention she was craving. She smiled and almost purred herself as he kissed her on the top of her head.

"Yes, it works," he conceded, giving another squeeze. Sebastian purred louder as he was gently crushed between them. "How are you feeling?"

She pushed her face into his chest, speaking directly into him. "Exhausted. Defeated. Cried out." The sound was muffled, and likely incoherent to Michael, but Lucas was used to her being – as she put it – 'cute.'

Lucas pulled her into his arms, listening to Sebastian's protests as he was crushed beyond his comfort, finally squirming free and skittering off. Lucas wrapped his arms around her and kissed her.

"I should have been there."

She squeezed him tighter. "One of us had to be responsible. How's Mabel been doing with my absence?"

"Stressed, but she gets it. She hates being without her right hand."

"Aw, you always say the nicest things."

Michael coughed from the doorway. "Whenever the two of you feel like breaking this up, I could go for that slice of pizza I was promised."

They laughed, and Cate broke the embrace, stealing

one more kiss before parting. "All right, you boys run out and get some beer; I'll call Papa Merrin's."

"Better be deep dish," Michael called back as he moved down the hall. "I didn't drag that monstrosity all the way up here for anything less."

Cate called back at him as she pulled out her phone. "Fine! But I get to pick toppings."

He groaned. "It's going to be barbeque chicken again, isn't it?"

"If I don't get my barbeque, I am ordering the Mediterranean."

"Artichokes don't belong on a pizza!"

She laughed and watched Lucas push Michael toward the door. "Negotiate your contract better next time!"

She heard the door close, and Cate drifted to the middle of the room, admiring the mirror. It *did* look like it belonged there – as if it were meant to be with her.

She stepped closer, flinching when she finally caught her own reflection's gaze. The dream – the *nightmare* – flashed to the forefront of her memory. She held herself as if to suppress an oncoming chill. She watched as the reflection mimicked her, its movement following her motions with precision. She imagined the reflection's heartbeat moving at the same rate, its molecules moving at the same pace and with the same rhythm as her own. The longer she stared, the more intrigued she was. The nightmare no longer held any fear for her. It was receding to the back of her mind, to be tucked away and soon forgotten.

"Hey! Earth to Cate!" She jumped, turning to the door where Lucas was staring at her. His brow arched across his forehead with curiosity. "Are you alright?"

"Fine." She stared at him, slowly turning and making her way to the jamb where he leaned.

"You sure? I've been asking if you called for pizza."

"Give me a minute, Mr. Impatient. You don't get to complain because you guys are so fast."

He stared at her. "Cate, we've been gone for thirty minutes."

Her eyes widened as she fumbled the phone already in her hand. She looked at the time. The evidence was there, even if she didn't understand: she had been standing in the bedroom for a half-hour staring into her own reflection.

"I don't understand..." She looked at the phone, shaking slightly.

Lucas reached out, drawing her in. "You've been driving for two days. I doubt you slept much while you were gone. You're probably jet-lagged –"

"I wasn't flying."

"Fine, *car*-lagged then. You're exhausted. You drove all that way, probably cried most of the time you were there, helped pack up your grandma's house, then loaded up that old mirror, and drove all the way back. It's no wonder you blanked out."

She slid her hands under his shirt, brushing them across his warm skin as she held him tight.

"I want things to go back to normal."

"This *is* normal now. You're going to get a good night's sleep and try out work tomorrow." He paused as if testing her tenuous grip on reality. "She's still going to be gone, Cate."

She didn't speak. His words hung on the air as they stood in the doorway.

"Eventually, you'll accept it as *your* normal and things will move forward. It's going to suck, but it'll get easier, little by little." He lifted her chin, smiling into her sad eyes. She refused to meet his gaze for a long moment.

"I'm going to be with you the whole way. We'll get through this."

He kissed her and she let the tears fall, smiling into the kiss. She tightened her grip on his waist, putting all of her faith into him and his confidence. He sounded so optimistic, so assured that everything would get back to normal so easily.

"Ahem."

They parted lips and turned to Michael, who was standing at the end of the hallway, seemingly unimpressed witnessing this situation yet again.

"Pizza is here. Thought you lovebirds would like to know."

She turned to Lucas as she wiped away the remnants

of her tears.

"You let him call for pizza?"

"Yep. Let him pick his own toppings, too."

Cate started into a glare, but waited, reserving judgment. Michael began to react with a glare of his own, then his eyes softened, and he broke into a small smile.

"Relax. It's barbeque."

NINE

Two slices of deep dish later, Cate could feel herself sinking into a food coma, folding into its cocoon of warmth. She leaned back into the plush couch cushions, trying to remain part of the conversation between Lucas and Michael. Slowly, she faded away from the lights and the conversation. Sebastian hopped onto her lap, curling up and purring loudly, sealing her fate as he raced her to sleep.

The sights around her faded away into a cloud of grey, disappearing into the dark behind her eyes. The sounds, first colorful and bright, lost shape and clarity; they dissolved into the same dark pool as she slipped away. Even the continuous vibration of her purring companion faded away into oblivion as she descended helplessly into the exhaustion that caught her.

When she opened her eyes again, Sebastian had abandoned her for more comfortable scenery somewhere else in the apartment. Lucas had either gone out with Michael or gone to bed, but left lights on for her to find her way by. She took her time, waiting on the couch until her faculties returned to her.

She looked around, smiling at the warm glow the lights provided. It was both comforting and comfortable. Waking up to it made her feel back at home and ready to rejoin the world she had so swiftly abandoned to familial duties. Part of her wanted to grab a blanket and curl up on the couch to sleep away the rest of the night, so she could wake up to the warm morning sun in her perfect living room. She considered it but decided she would rather wake up next to her beautiful man.

Cate stood too quickly, holding her arms out for balance as equilibrium swam elusively around her head. Hand over hand, she rounded the corner of the couch, her fingers tracing the edge of the end table as she circled the makeshift dining room behind the couch. She looked out the windows and jumped when she met her reflection. Mistaking it for a stranger in the dim room, her heart raced into a frenzy. Her reflection jumped back from her at the same time, panic in tandem. The mirrored action made it easier for her to catch her breath as she doubled over, perching her arms on her knees to keep herself on her feet. Once she found calm again, she righted herself, looking at her reflection and shaking her head in embarrassment. When had she become so jumpy? Had it started with Harriet's death? Or had it been building up and this was a manifested response to the trauma?

She laughed to herself, shaking her head again. The reflection seemed to agree with the sentiment: too much time was being spent in the psychology section at work.

Cate wondered her way through the apartment, back to the bedroom. She found her way by the light that trickled into the room from the hall. In the dim between the living room and the bedroom, she wormed her way out of her bra without bothering to remove her t-shirt – a skill that had always stunned Lucas. He always showed as much interest as confusion, as if it were a physical anomaly and not a task most women were capable of. She hopped out of her jeans, one leg at a time, and moved to the bathroom, closing the door before she flicked the lights on.

Teeth and hair both brushed, Cate applied her facial cleanser, feeling more human with every stage of the nighttime routine. Cate realized that Lucas was probably right: one decent night's sleep might actually put her back into the realm of normal human experience. She longed to be back among familiar feelings and thoughts.

She bent to the sink, splashing the warm water over her face to rinse the cleanser away. The warmth reminded her of what she was missing out on in the next room: warm, deep slumber, enveloped by her down comforter. She pulled the towel off the rack and smothered her face, patting the water away as she stood up. She pressed at her forehead, her cheeks, and her chin. She trailed the towel around her neck and then swept her hair back with the towel, whisking any stray moisture that might have threatened to disturb her peaceful sleep.

She double-checked herself in her reflection and stopped. Her reflection was looking back at her, but it was a cold, empty gaze that she was not projecting. On the other side of her mirror, her head was cocked at a disjointed angle, giving her an almost lizard-like quality as she regarded herself with blank, unfeeling eyes that were not her own.

She moved, wavering back and forth in front of the mirror, watching how her reflection didn't match the action. It only flicked its eyes unevenly: back and forth in a sharp movement, the reflection's gaze tracked Cate's rocking. Cate watched with the same intensity, her calm slipping away, leaving her suddenly aware of being half-naked and alone in the middle of the night. She hoped Lucas was on the other side of the door, but she couldn't know for sure. And if he were, what would she say?

Help! That's not me in the mirror! …but it was her, wasn't it?

She leaned closer to the mirror. The reflection leaned toward her. It was so much like her own reflection – except those eyes were not hers at all.

"W-what are you?" Its lips twitched but didn't part to mimic her. Was it mocking her? Did she detect the faintest sneer playing on the reflection's lips?

The question hung in the air unanswered for a long moment, drawn out on the silence of the night. Then, it seemed as if the reflection spoke. It was nothing Cate could hear, but its lips moved in the briefest way when Cate's definitely had not.

She shook her head and leaned closer. Its lips ran through the motions again, indistinct enough that Cate might never know what message was being relayed. Cate continued to close the distance on her side of the mirror, as it leaned in conspiratorially on the other side. Maybe, she reasoned, it could not hear her either. The glass between them might prevent clear communication. She watched the lips twitch a third time, in the strange small way that was entirely not her own. A third time, she heard nothing. She looked into its eyes, both their brows creasing in concurrent frustration, and Cate shook her head again.

"I can't hear –" But her words were cut off, ripping out of her throat in a scream as the mirror shattered in front of her, exploding outward as her reflection's glare burned into her.

She whirled backward, thrashing and yelling, covering her face and trying to protect herself from the diamond-sharp slivers. The fear ebbed long enough for her to realize that her hands and knees were not resting on the bathroom tile. The surface beneath her was soft, implying by the relative comfort that she must be out of harm's way. A canopy weighed on her and she pulled it back. This was definitely not the bathroom.

She was safe in bed, drowning in her oversized comforter, covered in a sheen of sweat. Cate sat up, looking around the room, her eyes darting from place to place.

It was morning, and she was alone.

She fell back onto the mattress, huffing out her frustration. The frustration boiling over inside at whatever was going on in her brain made her want to cry. Grinding the heels of her hands into her eyes, a growl erupted from within. She wanted to go back to sleep, but she didn't want to dream – nothing like that. There was little time this morning for anything else, anyway. She rolled over to look at the clock on the nightstand and immediately felt a cold chill.

She was supposed to be at work thirty minutes ago.

Returning to normal life was not going to be as easy as she hoped.

TEN

Lucas's chief responsibility was to open the store first thing in the morning – *every* morning. Usually, she was there to see him on his way, coffee already brewed and breakfast at the ready. With him already gone, and her inner clock on the fritz, no one was there to make sure Cate was up. No one made sure her day started on time, and no one rescued her from her nightmare.

Cate was never certain if the amount of time required to get ready in the morning multiplied because she was running late, or if it only appeared to do so because she was acutely aware of every moment wasted with the unnecessary.

This morning – her first day back to the regular grind after bereavement – was an awful indicator of the way the rest of the week might go. It was imperative to start the day off on the proverbial right foot. She had it in her head that a decent start was the only way she could reset her schedule, and her world, properly. It wasn't that Lucas's idealistic 'new normal' wasn't appreciated, but it was still too soon to accept.

Fortunately, she was only a bike ride away from the bookstore. Having an independent mode of transportation meant she didn't have to worry about traffic or bus schedules delaying her further. It was the mere matter of getting on the bike and pedaling like the wind. If the universe was kind, she might even make up time.

Cate scrambled around the living room, snatching up her bag and stuffing it with essentials. The phone rang; she knew without looking who would be on the other end. A glance confirmed that it was Lucas, and it was not his first attempt to reach her. She flicked the screen to answer the call, grabbing her keys as she moved to the door.

"I know. You don't have to say it."

"Actually, we're more worried than anything else."

"I'm fine. I overslept, that's all. Must be the lag you were talking about."

"Must be. When are you going to be here?"

"Ten minutes, I'm out the door already."

"Literally or figuratively?"

"Literally. I'm in the hall as we speak."

"Okay, be careful."

It was a slight relief to know that no one was crying havoc over her belated return. It was equally reassuring that her unexpected absence wasn't sewing dissent among her peers. Had they been slammed and she was needed but not present… she hated it when it happened to her. She swung a leg over the bike and pushed off, coasting down the slope that began her journey.

ELEVEN

The path between home and work was a mostly-even plane, but there were sloping side routes that made things more exciting. She considered a number of these detours, reminding herself that they didn't add much time, and it was usually easy to pick the route back up when the hills quit on her. In the end, Cate declined, deciding that distractions were not going to help her today, and only focus would get her there.

The sun seemed uncharacteristically warm as she raced out into the late morning, considering her luck that she hadn't overslept to the point of catching the lunch rush. The last time she got left behind in a noon rush, it had taken her almost the full hour to find her way back to the shop. At that point, it became company policy that lunch should be taken before or after the noon hour, but never during.

The air carried a chill with it that Cate blamed on the swiftness of her ride. She tried to ignore it, seeking the warmth as the breeze teased her hair, working the bedhead out of it. Two blocks from work, her luck ran out and she was forced to stop for traffic.

She waited, cars moving back and forth as a burning hand flashed, counting down from twenty on the pole across the street. Beyond the signal, she caught her reflection in a storefront window. It was holding her bike, an impatient foot on a ready pedal. Nothing noteworthy or out of place, but she could feel the muscles around her spine tightening as she watched. Minutes seemed to roll by as she waited to see it cock its head, revealing that she was no longer the owner of this reflection. Her reflection remained constant, and hers. The hand became a glowing person, and she carried on without another look, providing no more opportunities to unravel what was left of her jangled nerves.

She locked up the bike on a rack outside Mrs. Rogers' Neighborhood Bookstore, a tin bell rattled an alert as she opened the door and slipped inside. Lucas poked out from around the shelves, his mouth already open to welcome the would-be patron.

His face changed when he saw her. It became an uneven combination of delight and concern. He tried to reclaim his casual exterior, but it was not a feat easily accomplished.

From another aisle further removed, Rachel tittered with a friendly smile. Rachel was a hugger; everyone at the store accepted this was a thing – or learned to. There was no other option; it was her nature to express herself boisterously and, usually, physically as well. Once upon a time, the store crew tried to keep her from physically connecting with people; the experiment almost ruined her for the customer service industry. In the end, it was Lucas and a few of the part-timers who learned to adapt for her sake. There was nothing else to be done about it.

Cate, on the other hand, was all about hugs, especially from Rachel. It always seemed to her that Rachel's exuberance amplified everything good, and evaporated most bad things in it. She didn't expect her previous week of surprises and nightmares to simply evaporate – it wouldn't be that easy, she knew that. But a Rachel hug might start her on the road to where it would only get better, and she could get back to her uneventful life again.

Rachel hit the main aisle of the shop with a bright smile and open arms. She let out a squeal that communicated excitement without forgetting Cate's potentially fragile state. Rachel wrapped Cate into her slender arms, holding her close. Cate hugged back, feeling the gentle pressure envelope her.

For a long moment, nothing happened. Cate was

afraid she might be trapped with this feeling in her gut, but then came the warmth between them. Cate rested her head on Rachel's shoulder, the pained crease between her brows easing. Rachel offered a maternal coo and caressed the girl's hair.

"You poor thing. I know how much you loved Harriet."

Cate shook her head into Rachel's deep golden hair. She could practically feel Rachel sweeping the sadness and frustration away with each gentle caress. The sensation was so overwhelming, the words came without Cate's knowledge. "It's hard to believe she's gone. She knew and she didn't say anything."

"Oh hon, of course, she didn't. It would have been worse for you if she had. You would have been crying for days, maybe weeks before it ever happened." The moment was punctuated by Rachel giving a squeeze that dislodged the doubt and sent it rattling down to a place where it couldn't bother Cate for a while. "Instead, you have some sadness to deal with, but nothing to taint your memory of her. She spared you the memories of sick, frail, dying Harriet. Your memories will always be Harriet being Harriet."

She sniffled. "Stubborn to the bitter end."

"Like her granddaughter."

They tugged one another into a deeper hug, holding close for a full minute before Cate broke the embrace, smiling into the eyes of a girl who, despite the fact that she was five years younger than Cate, had the motherly instincts and maturity of a woman twice her age.

While they were hugging, Lucas had snuck in closer. He gave Cate a hug and a quick, semi-professional kiss on the cheek. He held her at arm's length scrutinizing, and she knew immediately he was inspecting her for signs of something.

"Everything okay?" He tried to mask his concern, but it was still there.

She tossed her hair around, her eyes rolling dramatically. "If you don't mean me being an idiot. I hope I didn't worry you too much."

He prodded her arm. "Only the undeniable revelation that you are only human."

Her mouth twisted with disapproval before she let a smile slip out. "I hate to think that I had misled you all this time. Wouldn't want you thinking I was a deity walking the earth among mere mortals."

Lucas shrugged, playing up the nonchalance. "It's fine; I'm sure there are other deities walking the earth that are deserving of my worship."

A fire sparked in her eyes then, first in surprise and then in defiance. Her arm extended before conscious command and connected with his arm. It had almost no effect physically, Lucas was already flinching away when he goaded her into attacking him, but the emotional upheaval did wonders for lightening the mood.

The laughter that ensued between the three of them was cut short by the sound of the office door creaking open. Mrs. Mabel Rogers, proprietor and namesake of the neighborhood store, poked her head out. She was not the sort to inspire fear or iron-fisted professionalism, but both Lucas and Rachel knew she had been waiting for Cate to come in. The silence painted an awkwardness that was definitely visible on all their faces.

"Cate, can we talk in my office, please?" She stood at the mouth of the aisle denoting the romance section, waiting for Cate to lead the way back to the office. Cate put on a muted smile when she made eye contact with Lucas and Rachel, smiling a little brighter for Mabel as she walked past.

Cate walked into the office. It was a large room made considerably smaller by the numerous filing cabinets taking up a good portion of the available space. This made the room seem abnormally long and tainted the sound quality with a strange echo that made conversations difficult with more than two people.

Mabel looked over cat-eye glasses, sliding them down her nose before taking them off completely. Earpieces clicked against the frame as they snapped closed, then hung from the chain that kept them close at hand. She returned Cate's muted smile and paused, almost holding her breath before speaking.

"How are you holding up?"

"It's an adjustment." Cate shrugged.

Mabel nodded in wordless agreement, her thick grey and brown ringlets bounced and shook as she agreed.

She leaned back in her chair a bit, gazing across the distance at Cate.

"Legally, you've used up your sick time. But you're my best employee," she smiled and leaned forward conspiratorially. "Don't tell the others."

Cate winked, but Mabel continued, "If you need more time, say so. I can't pay you for it, unfortunately, but take all the time you need. You'll always have a place here."

She stared at the older woman across the table and smiled wider, rubbing her eyes, caught somewhere between exhaustion, gratitude, and tearing up again.

"Thank you, really. But I think it's time I came back to work. I've spent so much time away already."

"The books aren't going to change if you take a little more time."

"But I might, and I don't want to. I want to get back to normal."

Mabel laughed. "You're welcome to try, but I haven't seen much normal around here ever."

"I know, but I have to start somewhere."

"Yes, you do." She flipped open her glasses and put them back on, drawing a notebook closer to her on the desk. "So, let's see what you've missed out on."

TWELVE

The rest of the day went by without incident. Customers came and went. Cate, Lucas, and Rachel ordered sandwiches from King's Deli around the corner; sandwiches made all the more delicious by the fact that Mabel would be joining them for lunch – a rare and welcome appearance outside her office during business hours. The fact that Mabel was buying had its own delightful impact on the meal.

Cate felt herself ease back into the routine and was almost disappointed as the day slipped quickly by. Lucas came from the back room, pushing his arms through the sleeves of a blue hoodie, adjusting as it hung from his broad shoulders.

"Do you want leftovers, or should I make my world-famous spaghetti tonight?" His eyes sparkled and he reached out, his fingertips dancing against hers.

Cate weighed her options, swaying in place as they had their exchange. It had only been a couple of days, but she had missed this. "Let's kill what's left of the pizza. You can make your amazing spaghetti later this week."

"World-famous," he corrected.

"It is not. And I am sure most of the world would have you shot if they knew your secret ingredient was–" His eyes widened cartoonishly as he reached out, clapping a hand gently over her mouth.

"Don't you dare! You are sworn to secrecy!"

She licked his palm, laughing as he reflexed. "Perhaps, but for the right price, I may have to sell out."

Lucas wiped his wet palm on his jeans. "You may find yourself a woman without a country."

Cate bit her lip, pulling him close. "I'm sure I can cut you a deal if you keep me. My skills are highly sought after."

His eyebrows rose as he leaned in, almost towering over her.

"Oh? And which skills are those?"

"Mister Stearns, your shift is over and you are distracting my help." The words were chiding but gentle, and only loud enough to catch them off guard. Mabel stood with a handful of supplies, moving from the office to the front desk where the register was located. "Go home. The two of you can trade double entendres later. In private later, like wholesome people."

She watched him over her glasses until he separated himself from Cate.

"Yes, Mrs. Rogers."

She stopped, pointing a pen tip at him. "There is no need for name-calling."

"Sorry, Mabel."

"Better." She nodded satisfactorily.

He smiled back and gave Cate a quick kiss. "I'll see you in a couple hours. Call if you need anything."

She whispered playfully. "If the warden will let me..."

He laughed with her, waving back to Rachel and Mabel.

"Good night, ladies."

The moment he was out the door, the other two women looked at Cate. They moved in close, circling her and cutting off any escape. It made her feel like a delicious little morsel reflected in their hungry eyes.

"Why don't you tell us why you're not sleeping well?" Rachel's voice sang the words as if something dirty were implied.

"What?" The bottom dropped out of her stomach, leaving her feeling cold and hollow. Cate wasn't sure she wanted to get into this with them, at least not yet.

"You're struggling to get through the day. Your hair is a mess, but you aren't fussing with it. You've got dark circles that look *almost* painted on." Mabel emphasized the word 'almost' as if casting enough doubt to give Cate a pass. She raised an eyebrow, challenging the girl to explain herself. "You're not our usual Cate, which implies that something else is going on."

Rachel tittered, "We're kind of hoping that it's something dirty and awesome. That would be better than what we are expecting to hear."

Rachel reached out and caressed Cate's shoulder for extra emphasis, in case it was precisely what they were expecting.

Cate thought of all the actual reasons for her erratic behavior, looking from one set of eyes to the other, then deciding the ground was much more worth focusing on.

"It's nothing."

"For the record," Rachel responded with hardly a pause in the conversation. "That's exactly what we were expecting to hear."

Mabel followed as if they'd rehearsed until there were no pauses at all in their routine. "It is not something we're going to accept, however."

Cate resigned herself, knowing that withholding anything from these two would make the remaining hours of work torturous.

"Okay, so it's not *nothing*, but it's not anything juicy." The silence told her that wasn't enough information. "I've been having nightmares."

The women looked at each other, then back at her.

"What sort of nightmares? How long?" Rachel inquired. She spent much of her downtime perusing the New Age section, consulting dream journals.

"It started two nights ago when I was heading home."

"And what are you dreaming about?"

Cate shook her head and leaned over the counter. Threading her fingers into her hair, she gave it a playful tug, hoping to yank the details out of her head.

"It's weird. They both took place where I fell asleep. Like the other night, I slept in the car, and last night in the apartment. Both times, the dream starts where I nodded off, so I don't realize it's a dream." A twinge of pain interrupts her thoughts, and Cate looks down to see she is wringing her own hands so tightly, her fingers are red. "I end up face-to-face with my reflection – but it's not me. I mean, it is, but it's not – it's like my reflection is possessed. Someone on the other side of the mirror wearing my face, pretending to be my reflection."

"Wearing your face? Like a Halloween mask?" Rachel stuck her tongue through her teeth and shook. Even as her tongue snaked back into her mouth, she suppressed another shudder. The description had clearly bothered her.

"No, more like... a body snatcher, I guess."

"Oh. Okay."

"Really!" She drew an outline on the table with her finger and hovered over it, seeing her head framed in the smeared surface of the polished table. Cate looked up, expecting Mabel and Rachel to understand what she was communicating. The two women looked between the table and Cate, a look of uncertainty in their eyes. She huffed. "It looked like me, and it moved like me, but then it would stop pretending. Like it wanted me to know it wasn't me – it wasn't my reflection anymore."

There was a long pause before Rachel continued the line of inquiry.

"And then what?"

"Then I woke up."

"It didn't do anything?"

Cate shook her head. "Not the first time."

"Okay, but the second time?"

"The mirror shattered, but it wasn't the reflection."

"Or was it?"

Cate wanted to refute the accusation but found that she couldn't. Rachel raised a finger as if to pause the conversation, then raced off, disappearing into her favorite section of the store. Mabel looked like she was trying to figure out what line of inquiry they wanted to follow next. They both stared after Rachel as she called out a couple more questions to Cate, finally emerging with three different books, setting them on the counter and flipping open the first one.

"Try not to bend the spines, or it's going to wind up in the used section and I'll take the difference out of your check." Mabel gave her workers plenty of leeway, but there were rules. The most important of them was not costing her any more money than they had to.

Rachel gave her a look. "I know, I know. If you only knew -" She stopped herself, looking sheepish.

"If I knew what?" Mabel looked down her nose at Rachel.

"Nothing!" She found the entry in the dream interpretation guide she was looking for. "Okay, mirrors often represent something reflected in our soul. So, if your mirror is dirty, maybe something you did makes you feel dirty."

"But it's not *one* mirror, it's *all* reflections. The first time it was in the car windows. Then, it was my bathroom mirror."

"I don't think it's specific to any one mirror, but let's see about that." Rachel flipped through one book while Mabel started looking through a second. Cate picked up the last that remained unconsulted and began to flip through it.

On a first pass, there were no specific passages about mirrors, so she read through the index and then flipped through a second time.

Mabel put her book down. "I don't think these books are going to be the help we are hoping for. This one, like yours," Mabel gestured to the other book, "Indicates that the mirror is more or less a metaphor for Cate's perception of herself."

Cate nodded, not necessarily in agreement but in understanding. She was ready to put her own book down when she stopped on a picture. It was a hand-drawn illustration depicting a person standing before a doorway. Through the doorway was another person. They were mirror images of one another; that much was undeniable in the illustration.

Cate put the book down and pointed at the picture, spine of the book be damned. Her finger dragged from the person standing in the doorway to a dark figure hiding behind the duplicate.

The passages in the chapter discussed dreams where a strange figure had taken the place of the viewer's reflection. It was interpreted as a sort of identity crisis, but Cate kept returning to the image. It wasn't an identity crisis. It was *something* pretending to be her reflection.

Rachel and Mabel continued their inquiry into the mysterious reflection in Cate's dream, refining the line of questioning in turns as they assisted last-minute customers. Beyond the illustration, the closest that Rachel could get was that Cate's dreams were warning her that she could be a danger to herself, which they all agreed seemed silly and inaccurate at best. Cate was an accidental danger to plenty of people, including Lucas, but not to herself, not even in her darkest times. She loved life with her whole being and had no appetite for self-destruction.

Rachel flipped the last book closed, putting it on the

pile. Together, she and Cate took them back to the shelves to be restocked, where they would likely sit until Rachel needed to consult them again.

"I don't know what to tell you, Cate. I'm not trying to minimize your struggle, but they seem pretty standard for nightmares. Probably related to… you know."

Cate nodded. She knew what Rachel was trying to say. Harriet's death was causing her stress that was developing into nightmares.

Cate put a hand through her hair, a sigh that ended in a small growl of frustration slipping from her lips. "I wish I knew where they came from and how to get them to stop."

"The stress will ease with time. So will the nightmares. Find your Zen and let it happen."

"That's easier said than done."

They returned to the desk where Mrs. Rogers herself was showing a guest around her Neighborhood Bookstore. Cate smiled; it made her think back to her first time in the store. She had wandered in looking for a book that the university didn't carry. She was still new to the area and hadn't wandered so far into downtown before. Mabel had been the only one near the front of the store and had honed in on Cate like a mama bird to a frightened fledgling. Before long, they were laughing over the storied histories of Cate's professors and she was already being welcomed into "The Neighborhood" by the other two working that day. Little did Cate know, her talk with Mabel had turned into an interview without her knowledge. Cate started working for Mabel before the week was done. Then would come the fateful day she met Lucas. The rest would be history.

Mabel walked the customer to the door and flipped the sign out front from Open to Closed. There was still more than an hour before closing. Cate raised an eyebrow, watching the matron as she turned the lock on the door and gave it a test push. Turning, Mabel looked back at both girls eyeing her suspiciously.

"It's been a long day; Cate isn't quite ready for a full shift. Rachel, why don't you walk her home."

"I think I can manage that." Rachel turned to grab her things from the back room. Cate held Rachel in place.

"You don't have to –"

Mabel gave her the same look she offered Lucas earlier for calling her "Mrs. Rogers." "I will do whatever I please. It's my store and you are my minions. Now go home and take Rachel with you."

Cate smiled and listed slowly, backing toward the front door, giving Rachel time to gather her possessions. "Okay. Thank you, Mabel."

"Thank me by getting a good night's rest."

"I will."

Rachel grabbed Cate by the elbow and dragged her back through the store. They proceeded through the exit and Rachel pulled it closed behind them, twisting the lock closed again, her keys dropping easily back into her pocket. Rachel kept her composure until they had rounded the block completely, passing beyond the view of the store before her fist shot out in exclamation.

"Out early! Bless you, Cate!" She grabbed Cate's head in both her hands and kissed her temple with a loud cartoonish "mwah."

Wiping her face, Cate staggered out of Rachel's grasp with a small laugh. "You are an idiot. We have the best job in the world and you don't like being there."

"It's not that I don't like the job; I don't like the late hours. It's always too dark when we close up and I don't ever feel safe walking home alone."

"You need to get a bike – dammit!"

"What?"

Cate wanted to throttle herself for being so distracted. "My bike. I left it at the store."

"Let's go back for it."

"No, it'll take us even longer to get home if we double back now."

"You're going to have to make sure you get up on time tomorrow."

Cate let a huff of air escape her. "Earlier, since I'll be walking."

* * * *

The conversation continued; rambling topics

discussed throughout the day wound around to topics that couldn't usually be talked about because of other ears listening.

"He goes a little crazy when you're not around. You know that, right?" Rachel blurted out into the quiet street. It didn't startle Cate, but that didn't mean she knew how to respond to it.

"What, like strippers and drugs? Or more like *The Shining?*"

"No, I mean, he doesn't really know what to do with himself when you're not around. He gets mopey and he stays in mostly. He's like a puppy. He's a good guy and he misses the hell out of you. It's adorably sad; you're pretty much his whole world."

Cate smiled and wrung her fingers, leaning into Rachel. Some small part of her agreed that it was sad and she should be ashamed that he suffered like that when she wasn't around. Her heart, however, did a million cartwheels knowing that she had found such a rare and delightful creature to fall in love with.

"He's got Michael, too, you know. He's hardly lonely."

Rachel made a face. "Michael is a mongoloid and he belongs in a museum."

They laughed for a full minute. Cate at the direct aggression on display, Rachel because Cate's laughter was always infectious.

"Mostly, Michael tries unsuccessfully to get Lucas to

do things when you're not around. But it is good that he has friends to look after him."

As if the conversation had been timed for precisely that moment, they reached their parting. From this corner, Rachel and Cate were exactly the same distance from home. They hugged and parted ways, leaving Cate with her thoughts and Rachel's words.

When she got in, Lucas was sprawled across on the couch, reading. Sebastian lounged on the back of the couch, looking sleepy but perturbed that his favorite spot was currently occupied. All feline thoughts of displeasure evaporated the moment she came in the door. She hefted him into her arms as he scrambled over to her. Cate caressed him, holding him close as she moved over to the place where Lucas sat on the couch.

"You're early. I wasn't going to start dinner for a bit yet."

She put Sebastian down and held Lucas's chin, lifting his face to her as she leaned down to kiss him. She kissed him hard, pouring her emotions out into that one moment. She kissed him for all the things Rachel told her. She kissed him for all the moments she missed out on doing so – and all the moments she might miss in the future. She kissed him for all the sad, selfish reasons she wished he'd been with her for her difficult trip back home – and she realized that even though it was selfish, it wasn't entirely.

Cate took Lucas's book, closing it with a snap before

setting it on the end table, not breaking the kiss as she straddled his waist. Following her lead, he held her firmly by the hips, leaning deeper into the kisses. She smiled against his mouth and helped him out of his shirt.

Sebastian watched this entanglement with a continued, deepening displeasure. First, his favorite spot had been stolen. Now, it was clear that he would not be getting it back for some time.

At least this meant the bed was empty.

THIRTEEN

Cate woke slowly and stretched, her feet hitting the arm of the couch and pushing her slightly up the cushion before she stopped. She opened her eyes and looked around the brightly lit room.

Morning. The sight of sunlight streaming in through the windows as it stretched across the floor made her skin prickle with perceived warmth. It was early, maybe even *too* early. As she stretched, she found that she had more than enough space on the couch. Lucas had beaten her out of bed, but that didn't mean she was late – but too late to enjoy waking up next to him.

She closed her eyes again, letting herself swim in the half-sleep of morning. She lingered in the space where she was awake enough to identify the sounds around her, aware of time passing, but not so much that she could no longer enjoy lying on the couch with her eyes closed.

She half expected Sebastian to be curled up against her – or *on* her – purring away, but she did not feel his furry warmth anywhere. He might have been taking advantage of the sunlight that often streaked across the lower half of the bed. Cate always felt the late morning sun made the bed too warm for sleeping in unless she moved parallel to the sunlight. The issue with sleeping across the bed was Lucas's insistence that she warn him, instead of her suggestion to "go along with it," as she so often replied to his protests.

Lucas was of the opinion that when you were up, you were up. He would delay his day until it was necessary. Cate liked to have time to ease into her day. Sebastian was her coach in all things. According to his teachings, there was little that could not be done while lounging half-asleep. Cate had seen Sebastian do most things at that speed. She was not the Olympic-level snoozer he was, but that didn't mean she couldn't appreciate his approach to things.

She peeked again, monitoring the room for any signs of life. There didn't appear to be anything moving or breathing in the vicinity. No sounds of breakfast – not even Lucas's enthusiastically loud consumption of cereal. She also noticed that there were no sounds or smells of coffee, which was simply unheard of – unless he was in the shower. Had she woken up with him and not realized it? She pondered the thought, her eyes sliding closed again.

She must have fallen asleep again because the next thing she knew, Lucas was shaking her shoulders, trying to wake her.

No, not trying to wake her. And not Lucas.

Her brow pinched as she felt the hands roll her off her shoulder, moving her flat on her back. Rough hands pressed her into the couch. She opened her eyes to ask Lucas what he was doing and choked on a scream. She was looking up at herself, and she was leaning over her.

No, not her. Not Cate. This was someone else – some*thing* else.

It looked like her, almost exactly, but there was something in its eyes, or something missing from them. She couldn't pin down precisely what made them different, but the thought dropped away from the front of her mind. There were more pressing matters at hand.

Cate reached up, intent on pushing the impostor back and getting to her feet. Her reflection had other plans and grabbed her wrists, holding them over the arm of the couch in one tightly clamped hand.

Cate winced as her bones ground against one another, pinching her skin between them. She couldn't help but cry out. No sooner did the sound escape her lips – a feeble yelp – her doppelgänger straddled her. It moved with snake-like grace, its spine bending and twisting as it lowered its face to hers.

"What do you want?" Cate wished the words sounded stronger. They slipped out on the crest of a whimper. She knew they couldn't be interpreted as anything but weakness and fear. Still, she didn't let her shuddering voice stop her desire to understand. "Why are you doing this?"

It paused regarding her, and Cate could see the difference between them. The creature wearing her face did not blink. Its eyes weren't dead, but they didn't sparkle with life. They didn't tic back and forth as they took in new information. Its eyes simply stared at her, into her. Then it did something else.

Cate didn't understand what she was seeing. At first, it was almost unnoticeably different, then twisted into something freakish and grotesque. It hovered over her, holding her down as it cocked its head, giving her a lopsided stare. Its lips grew taut, muscles pulling at the sides of its mouth from somewhere within. They pulled until the pink flesh cracked, glistening red with thin lines of blood. Muscles continued to flex, its mouth stretching until its lips ripped, tearing like a split seam in fabric, exposing the mottled pink flesh beneath. Its lips parted, stretching across white teeth immediately streaked with blood, cheeks looking like hamburger as it tilted its face from one angle across to the other.

Cate's stomach twisted with understanding, a sour spoil rising in her throat.

It's trying to smile.

The thought crept through her mind, sending a twinge of fear down her spine. Cate knew that was exactly what she was seeing. It was holding her down, studying her, and trying to learn her mannerisms. She shook her head and pulled against her captor, trying to fight for leverage. The entire time, it gyrated over her, mimicking her, trying to capture her movements.

"No! You can't be me! I won't let you!"

She managed to pull one hand free, feeling nails cut into her flesh as she pulled. She screamed. It was a sound that started quivering and pathetic, transforming with the arc of her arm, becoming fierce and primal. Her anguish turned into anger, adding strength to the swing as she brought her fist down on her mimic's shoulder. It wasn't a crushing blow, but it stunned. She used the moment to shift her weight, rolling her assailant off the couch and to the ground. Certain that every second mattered, she pulled herself up, grabbing the lamp from the end table and pulled hard, feeling the power cord snap free. She turned, barely on her feet, shaking and scared. Another scream boiling in her throat, as Cate hoisted the lamp over her head, ready to crack its face open to see what lay beneath.

"Cate, please! Stop!"

She half-turned, ready to defend her actions to Lucas. That she would not stop and she would not surrender. But Lucas was not where she expected to see him. She turned the other way; he was not in any direction she looked. For one moment, she hesitated and the thing beneath her scrambled away. She raised the lamp again and faltered.

"Lucas?"

He was on the floor, his hair still wet and tousled, fresh from the shower. He was in his boxers, holding his shoulder. She could already see a reddened area spreading over the skin – a mark left from clobbering her loving boyfriend.

Fury gave way immediately to shock, the lamp tumbling to the floor and shattering in front of her. She stumbled backward, grabbing the couch for support, oblivious to the scattered ceramic edges biting into her soft flesh. She looked around again, certain this was some kind of trick. She felt like this must still be part of the dream – another awful dream. Any moment now, as soon as she dropped her guard, rushing in to make sure Lucas was okay, it would return and she would wake up in a cold sweat, screaming and shaking and wishing it had never happened. But she was lucid now – she was aware and it would not get the drop on her.

She snatched up a large shard from the broken lamp from the floor and waved it in front of her.

"Stay back."

"Cate, you were having a nightmare. It's over now. You're awake. Please, put that down before you hurt yourself."

She shuffled backward as he pulled himself slowly to

his feet. For her benefit, he kept his hands out in front of him so she could see. He spoke calmly, concerned, like Lucas would.

She shook her head slowly, not taking her eyes off him.

"I will put it down when I know I am safe."

He gestured to her feet. She could see footprints in dark red as she stepped out of them. She didn't feel any pain, so it had to be part of the dream, another trick.

"Cate, you're hurt. Let's get you off your feet –"

She lunged forward, swinging the shard at him, tightening her grip on it. "Get back! It's my life; you can't have it!"

His eyes pleaded with her as she backed away; short, hurried steps down the hall.

"Cate, please! This isn't a dream!"

She paused in the bedroom, sliding the door shut. Before it could close fully, she yanked it back open, changing her mind as she darted for the bathroom, locking the door behind her.

She caught a glimpse of her own reflection in the mirror and reacted on pure instinct. She slashed, the ceramic shard skating along the smooth surface. Her arm followed through and she cried out as her hand collided with the wall, the ceramic shard splintering under Cate's crushing grip. Her hand lit with pain, numerous slivers driving into her palm and fingers. Between the splinters digging into her hand and her sudden awareness of the pain in her feet, Cate understood with frightening clarity that she was not dreaming. She tried to hold her bleeding hand in the other, only to find the pain was worse. She held her wrist, backing against the wall and sliding down, pinned between the toilet and the tub.

The tears streamed freely for so many reasons all at once. For the pain, for fear of sanity abandoning her, for fear of what she might have done to Lucas if he had not cried out, for what she might do to either of them at any point in the future.

The door handle rattled. Lucas pounded from the other side. "Cate? Are you okay? Cate, please, open the door!"

She wanted to say that she couldn't, that she was going to sit here and wait for everything to be okay. Instead, she could only sob louder.

"I'm coming in. Please, Cate. I swear it's me. We can talk this out."

She nodded, even though she knew he couldn't see her. He hit the door a couple of times. It crackled and bounced, but did not give. He attacked it again, the knob rattling in its casing. The door splintered on the third kick and with the fourth, it heaved inward, embedding itself in the drywall. Lucas was breathless; the effort apparently more than he expected. He was trying to keep his composure, to appear calm and collected. But when he saw the scene laid out before him, he unraveled. Tears welled in his eyes as he came in, kneeling in front of her. He held her wounded hand delicately, hearing her cries rise, even as gingerly as he handled her. He released her arm, letting her support her wrist and put his arm around her shoulders. His other arm slid under her knees and slowly, they rose, Lucas carrying Cate with him. Together, they left the bathroom, each a little worse for wear on such a beautiful morning.

FOURTEEN

Cate spent most of the day in bed, drifting through a dreamy unreality. She slipped in and out of conversations that she may or may not have actually been a part of; she couldn't say for sure. She remembered everyone hovering around her at one time or another. Lucas, Rachel, Michael – even Mabel was there, though Cate couldn't say for sure if any of them had *actually* been there.

One thing she understood clearly was the pain surging through her hand. It felt like it had been dipped in lava. Twice she felt required to look at it to confirm it was not, in fact, on fire. It had been bandaged very well. She wasn't sure who deserved that thanks; she wasn't sure any of her friends had First Aid training. She noticed areas of the gauze wrapping tinged pink, the areas darkening, seeping through as the day progressed. She resigned her day to the people in her life, allowing them to take the reins. She had no desire to be in charge anymore. She wasn't sure she wanted to be part of it at all.

Sometime in the late afternoon, when the sun was still bright but no longer visible from their apartment, her hand lit up like Christmas. She gritted her teeth and tried to ignore it, willing herself someplace far away from the pain. When the power of positive thinking didn't work, she got onto her feet – now reminded of the pain in them as well. She hobbled her way around the apartment in search of Lucas, or pain pills, whichever she found first, though she hoped they were together. Her feet radiated pain somewhere beneath her shaky knees. They had been bandaged with the same skill as her hand but continued to hurt with each step. It was slow going and painful as she braced the wall with her only capable limb, the distance down the hall seeming so much further than it had been the day before.

As she neared the living room, she could hear Lucas and Rachel having a hushed conversation not meant for her.

"She's been muttering all day, saying the strangest damn things."

"Yesterday at work, she said she's been having nightmares."

"She was thrashing around like it was a nightmare. She

fought me when I tried to wake her. When she finally did wake up, she looked like she was going to kill me."

Cate shook her head as she stood, listening. They were retracing her steps, but they didn't get it. They were both convinced that this was a nightmare, and Cate was overreacting. But she wasn't trying to hurt Lucas; she was defending herself from a monster.

"But she stopped."

"She thought she was still dreaming, and I was some impostor. That's when she locked herself in the bathroom."

"And attacked the mirror."

"Yeah."

Then it was quiet. She waited, hoping they would discuss the rest of the day, so she could decipher what had been real and what had not.

"She's not taking Harriet's death well at all."

"I knew they were close, but I can't believe any tragedy could do this to someone."

"I'm not crazy."

They both turned, moving around the couch quickly. Rachel came to one side while Lucas flanked her on the other. They both helped her shuffle to the couch, cooing sympathies to her as if she hadn't heard the conversation.

Once she was seated, they helped to elevate her feet. Lucas held her legs while Rachel slid an overstuffed pillow under them. It was probably the only time Cate would ever keep quiet about feet on her coffee table. She leaned back into the couch, trying to make herself comfortable but felt the tension coursing through her muscles, distrust for every shadow and unseen threat in the living room singing in every nerve.

Rachel and Lucas hovered, their voices straining to sound upbeat.

"Feeling better?"

"Can we get you anything?"

They both stood waiting, beaming sympathy.

"I'm not crazy."

Lucas's smile faded. He sat next to her, naturally reaching for her hand and stopped, his palm hovering over the bandages and altered his plan to rest his hand on her thigh instead.

"No one said you were. But something is going on."

Cate could feel the tears boiling behind her eyes. She wanted to cry out in frustration and anger. Of course, something was going on; did they think she was blind to it? She was at the center and though she had no idea what it was, it was *not* a psychotic break.

"I don't think it was Harriet's death. I don't think it's my brain." She paused, thinking about the documentaries she watched about brain tumors that made people go crazy and do all kinds of awful things. She rubbed her eyes and sighed. "I *hope* it's not my brain."

She winced as her hand surged with pain again, cradling it like a wounded animal. Lucas relinquished his seat to Rachel as he disappeared to the kitchen, glasses clinking as he moved around. Rachel eased an arm around her, resting her head against Cate's.

"Whatever is going on, we are here for you – all of us."

She thought of her fever dreams from earlier. "Was... Mabel here?"

"She didn't even hesitate. She ran out the door with me as soon as Lucas called. She's been calling every hour for updates. She'll be delighted to hear you are doing better."

Lucas returned with a glass of water and two chalky white pills. Cate didn't bother to ask what they were. She took them gratefully with the water, feeling the cool trickle soothe aches she didn't realize she had.

Lucas took the glass from her and gestured to her hand. "Mabel called in a favor from one of her friends down at the Ready Clinic."

Rachel looked a little ill and cleared her throat. "They pulled over a hundred slivers out of your hand and feet. It's a wonder you're not in more pain."

They talked for a while longer. Cate switched to coffee, deciding that she had plenty of sleep for one day. She relaxed on the couch with Sebastian, trying in vain to get some reading done. She even took a call from Mabel, who reminded her that whatever was going on, she was there to help in any way she could.

"No questions asked," Mabel added. "Anything you

need."

Cate realized that she was not only loved; she was needed. Not in the exemplary employee fashion, but she was needed in their lives as much as she needed all of them in hers.

* * * *

A day of lazing about turned out to be its own test of her sanity. More than once, she tried to disprove her helplessness, but preparing dinner was not one of the ways she was going to be helpful – even reheating leftover pizza. Instead, she hobbled back to the bedroom to change. Michael was coming over. She could at least prove to her friends that she was capable of dressing herself. It was slow work, only having one hand get ready with, but she found that she could at least avoid the pain in her feet by walking on her tiptoes.

She opted for something loose-fitting. Preferably a top that would conceal the fact that she could not fasten a bra one-handed. After the ordeal of trying to put on panties with one hand, she also concluded that snaps and zippers were out. Leggings would have to do.

She finished tugging and twisting, almost positive that everything was settled where it belonged. She double-checked herself in the mirror, turning this way and that. Finally, she nodded, satisfied she had managed the impossible and rewarded herself with one final victory twirl. She spun like a ballerina, her head remaining focused, almost motionless, until her neck reached its limit and snapped around to the same point on the other side.

Immediately, she planted her feet, ignoring the pain and staring hard at her reflection in the antique mirror. For a moment, it seemed that her reflection had not been able to keep up, like she had been watching her reflection move on a slight delay. Perhaps it was the pain medication, with all the movement going on in the twirl, but panic seized at her heart, afraid she was slipping into another nightmare. She turned again, watching more intently, but saw nothing out of sorts.

Cate hesitated a moment longer, then tiptoed her way back to the living room, forcing herself to not look back at her reflection. Skin and small hairs prickled on the back of her neck, begging her to turn around, desiring one last look. She fought the need; nothing good would come of knowing she was being watched.

FIFTEEN

The rest of the night carried on like an ordinary dinner party. Cate felt more of herself coming through with every laugh, every story, and every refill of her wine glass. They carried on well after the wine was depleted, Michael and Rachel finally deciding that it was past Cate's bedtime and Lucas should do his part in enforcing a schedule.

Cate laughed, but she also heard the underlying message. One of Rachel's many goals was to goad Cate into pregnancy. Rachel hated dating; she didn't believe that any man out there could match her towering expectations, so she lived vicariously through Cate. At least, she tried. It was difficult to force Cate to live a life Rachel wanted, especially when it didn't adhere to Cate's own whims. But Rachel had gotten to a point where she assumed she was too old to complete her bucket list on her own, so she attempted to have it completed on her behalf.

It was the way Cate and Lucas were – serious, committed, endearing. Rachel hadn't found that and was convinced she never would. Instead of working on her own life, she tried to manage Lucas and Cate. No matter how many times Cate tried to explain it, Rachel couldn't comprehend why Cate wasn't interested in getting pregnant on Rachel's insistence.

"But you love kids." Rachel's argument always started the same way. As did Cate's defense.

"*Other people's* kids."

"But your kids would be awesome."

"Yes, they will - later."

"But *I* want you to have kids *now.*"

"I am not putting my body through that yet."

"Then why don't you adopt?"

"Because I don't want kids right now. Not mine, and not anyone else's." Cate often ended the conversation at this point, signaling with an accusatory finger, ceasing any further questioning.

Tonight, she didn't even let the conversation begin. The moment they were up, she loaded items into her one good hand and walked them to the kitchen. The cleaning could wait till morning as long as the organizing was done tonight.

Lucas ushered their guests to the front door where he

wished them well. Cate could almost hear the whispers.

Make sure Cate is okay tonight – as if Lucas were oblivious without their reminding. She had to tamp down her annoyance. They worried, and she understood why. Cate was hoping for a nightmare-free slumber, too. She hadn't managed one since she got back.

Lucas closed the door behind him, leaning against it. He wasn't drunk, but it looked like every bit of movement required an extra effort behind it.

Their eyes met and she smiled. Lucas smiled back; it was slower but broader. Maybe he was a little drunk.

"I think it's time I took you to bed."

Her words drifted to his ears and he almost glided away from the door. He made it look so easy, drifting to the couch and leaning over it. She tried her best to saunter, leaving the kitchen on pained feet as she watched him pat the cushion. She couldn't look at the couch without remembering –

She reached out, snatching up her glass and gulping down what remained of the wine. She skirted the table too tightly, uneven on her occasional tiptoes. She bumped the corner of the table and over-corrected, spinning, her arms pinwheeling. Fortune smiled for once, and she landed hard on the couch, her head all but resting on his lap, mere inches from where he had asked her to sit down.

Whether he didn't notice the gaffe, or didn't comment on it, Cate couldn't say. He leaned over, kissing her forehead, then chin, then her mouth, all upside down. The wine made the sensation into something new and electric. She smiled against his mouth. "Help me up, please."

He obliged, assisting as she rose to her feet. One hand in hers, the other around her waist, they moved into the hall together.

"I may need help changing out of these clothes." She squeezed his hand gently as they moved into the dark room.

"I thought you would never ask."

SIXTEEN

Cate woke to sunlight on one cheek and a purring hindquarter on the other. Sebastian was known to slip into the bed and sleep on their pillows. Often, he would rest in the crook of her neck, or curl up at the top of her head like a crown. Apparently, he decided sometime during the night that nuzzling would cure whatever ailed Cate – and really, one end was good as the other when it came to nuzzling. Sebastian was, fortunately, soft, furry, and full of love from end to end. It was occasionally hard to tell which end was which when he was curled up. Cate had nuzzled back, thinking she was rubbing against his head, or perhaps his shoulder. She didn't understand her mistake until Sebastian's tail flicked with approval. The realization caused Cate to cry out, both in shock and laughter. The sudden riot brought Lucas running, only to find pleasantries awaiting him instead of nightmares and panic.

He came into the room slower, his composure returning to him. Long breaths and slow steps helped him gather his own calm. Cate sat up, watching his calm slip away again as the sheets shifted and she reminded him what she wore to bed.

"Problems getting around this morning?" Lucas sat on the edge of the bed; a leg folded beneath him. He traced his fingers over the soft fabric of the bedsheet, outlining her leg beneath.

She walked her fingers down to his hand, where they teased before finally lacing into his.

"No, not really, except for waking up with a face full of cat butt."

They shared a laugh, and she fell back, rolling out of her molded place in the mattress. She stretched and yawned, moving much like her feline companion at the start of any given day. She twisted her head to smile up at Lucas, her eyes glittering, fully aware that his thoughts were not driven to such naughty places watching Sebastian paw around on the bed. He smiled, awkwardness creeping across his face.

"Um, Mabel, wants you to take the day off. And," He sighed, looking as uncomfortable as he could in his own skin. He was clearly caught between business and pleasure. "I'm doing the morning shift, so I can be here at night."

Cate bit her lip and rolled over again, looking at him upside down. "I think you're going to be late to work." She reached out, tugging at his arm and drawing him closer.

"I am definitely going to be late to work." He crawled into bed without having to be told a second time.

SEVENTEEN

When Cate woke again, the morning sun had been relieved by its afternoon counterpart. She got up slowly, working through her stretch and yawn – this time without any distracted admirers.

She threw on a robe and Lucas's discarded pajama pants, making her way slowly to the kitchen. She started a pot of coffee and clambered up on the counter, resting her feet while she waited for it to brew.

It amazed her how difficult her daily life became by removing a single hand from the equation. It never occurred to her until she lost the use of one. The simple act of pouring a cup of coffee was a two-handed process most days. She could – and did – pour a cup of coffee with one hand, but it was tedious. Get the mug off the hook, put the mug down, pick up the pot, pour the coffee, put the pot down, pick up the sugar, pour the sugar, put the sugar down, find a spoon, stir the coffee, add some milk, stir the coffee, taste the coffee, add more sugar...

The tedium made her head hurt – almost as much as her bandaged hand when she forgot and grabbed for something with it. It wasn't that there was a right or wrong way to grab hold; her hand was covered in countless cuts, ranging from slight to severe and every time she grabbed hold of something, the pressure threatened to open them all up again. She was sure at least a few of them already had; she would have Lucas take a look when he got home.

Cate enjoyed a cup of coffee from her view atop the kitchen counter, much to Sebastian's disapproval, as he was never allowed up there. She treated herself to a second cup of coffee on the living room couch, where the Maine Coon much preferred her – as long as she continued to pet him.

Her mind drifted through the afternoon, feeling levity begin to restore itself after a decent night's slumber. It was strange what one terror-free night could do for the disposition. Cate felt ready to tackle the world – if she could only find the motivation to get off the couch. Running her fingers through her matted hair seemed to be exactly the motivation she needed. Regular wear and tear combined with additional strain through activities with Lucas, she discovered a frightful mess resting on her scalp. Cate decided that, for her own safety, a bath might be in order.

She shook her head and tried not to laugh too hard at herself as she tucked three of her limbs into plastic sandwich bags, wrapping them in cling wrap up to the joint. She considered the humiliation she faced alone far better than whatever fate awaited her if she wandered around in soaked bandages – or worse, none at all. If she could keep her own mouth shut, no one would even know.

Cate waited until the water was hot – so hot that she turned it back to make sure there was actual water pouring out of the showerhead, and not steam alone. Satisfied, she stepped carefully and sat down, letting the water beat down on her. The heat worked its way into her muscles, melting away her cares as she inched into the water, twisting slowly and letting out audible approval as the stress flowed out of her body and down the drain. She reached up, prodding at the showerhead to move the selector to a pressure massage. She leaned her head against the wall, feeling the water beat into her shoulders, kneading away the knots where Cate carried her stress.

Cate stayed under the water until the temperature slipped beneath scalding. For anyone else, it be hot enough still, but for Cate, only the feel of disfiguringly high temperatures soaking into her muscles would do when she was trying to relax and recover.

She shut off the shower and stood carefully, the water tracing rivulets down her form as they raced each other for the drain. Pressing her hands to her scalp, she squeezed the water from her hair down her spine to join the exodus.

She pushed the curtain back and stepped out of the bath, pulling a towel from the corner shelf where one of her favorites – a plush purple blanket of a towel – rested on top of the stack. Shaking it out, it wrapped her shoulders like a royal cape. The heat from her body transfer to the towel, trapping it against her skin a bit longer. One at a time, Cate released her arms and trapped the towel under them, wrapping it tightly and tucking the fabric inside itself. Once her arms were free, she set to extricating herself from the plastic traps she had created.

She wrestled with the plastic wrap around her arm first, twisting her head in strenuous frustration while she pulled at the random lengths of twisted plastic, though it did nothing to advance her effort. Growling and gritting teeth didn't seem to have any effect on the plastic's resistance either, but it made her feel like she was putting forth her best effort. The longer Cate worked at disentangling herself, the more she floundered, the effort becoming more of a performance. During her struggle, she caught sight of something in her periphery. Thinking something might have passed outside the small window they used for a vent, Cate waited, motionless, but nothing happened. She turned in place, feeling a twist of cool air on her warm skin and indulged herself, swaying slowly as she pushed the air gently around her. It took another minute before realization sank in. Cate continued to watch, disbelieving, swaying slowly, watching closely. The horror that initially threatened to overwhelm ebbed away and was replaced by a curiosity that bordered on the comical.

The mirror, always too close to the shower itself for any practical use right after, glistened with a coat of heat mist from her ages-long shower. The mist was layered so thick she couldn't actually see herself, but if she looked off-center, she could see the opaque shadow that matched her mirrored shape. As she swayed, it became clear that her reflection – if she dared call it that – could not keep up with her movements. With each gesture Cate made, there was a moment's hesitation before the reflection followed. Whatever was happening, whatever this thing was on the other side of the mirror, it was not all-powerful. Cate's chest tightened; she was caught between two bizarre sensations. It was real; her nightmares were real and here in the room with her in the middle of the waking day. Better, it had a weakness and, almost comically so, she found it. That weakness gave Cate hope, for once. Weakness meant that, with a little luck, it could be beaten.

Hope ebbed again with the rest of her emotions. Cate hoped that luck was on her side, as the issue at hand now floated to the top of her priorities. Glass, dimensions, and who knew what else separated Cate from her enemy. She needed to know more if she was going to conjure up a way to beat it.

EIGHTEEN

All day, Cate planned her discussion with Lucas. It seemed blurting it out was the easiest way, but when he finally got home, she couldn't put it out there.

"Hey, I'm not crazy," didn't open the conversation the way she wanted it to.

"It's more of a demonic possession thing," also did little to reinforce her position.

Cate decided that the best option was to leave well enough alone until she had more answers. Broaching the subject would only lead to more questions; it was best to quit while she was ahead – for the moment, anyway.

There was no simple way to make Lucas understand that, whatever this thing was, it had picked *her*. Not without sending him into one panic or another. Cate needed answers. It chose to look like *her* – did it want to *be* her? Whatever it was trying, she would fight it; she would stop it. But they were not at that crossroad yet. She pushed the thought from her brain, trying to focus on the present.

They spent a quiet night on the couch, watching awful movies on-demand. Half her attention was on the movies, but the rest was on her dreams. What if it was her brain? But no, she couldn't second guess herself like that. If she started doubting her sanity now, no one would be there to defend her in the end. This was not her doing. Lucas put an arm around her and she flinched. He withdrew and Cate realized at once how tense she'd been all night.

"Did I… do something?" He was hesitant, trying to be comforting and supportive, but distant in case that was what she needed. Lucas was usually good at giving her options. Sometimes, he was so thoughtful, it annoyed her.

"Yes! No," Cate took a breath and expected to have more to say. Instead, she deflated. "I don't know. I…"

"Hey," he cupped one of her hands in his, giving it a squeeze. "Whatever you need."

She smiled meekly, both appreciating the gesture and still frustrated with a situation she couldn't even talk to him about.

"I'll be alright."

She curled into him and he leaned into the side of the couch. Cate sighed, finding the comfort that was there and ignoring everything else.

Lucas nodded off first, having actually exerted himself during the day, while Cate had followed Sebastian's lead: lounging, perching, and sleeping most of the day away. She drew the line at bathing herself in the living room.

She leaned into Lucas, smiling as she felt his heartbeat drum against her ear, enjoying the rhythmic rise and fall of his chest. Each breath, each beat lulled her further into a gentle sleep against him as he snoozed, his cheek nestled into the palm of his hand. It was quiet and warm and Cate never felt herself take that final dive into slumber.

* * * *

Cate woke abruptly, startled awake, but unaware of what by. Her eyes scanned the room, but nothing seemed out of place. It occurred to her that, with no apparent cause for her waking, a new nightmare may have begun. Already, this one separated itself from the others: Lucas there, still asleep on the couch. She rubbed her eyes, wondering if that meant she was awake. If it wasn't a dream, what woke her?

She looked around the room, but nothing was amiss. It wasn't unreasonable that, in his quest to find the most comfortable sleep, Sebastian had knocked something over. However, nothing appeared out of place. Lucas's skull still rested in his palm, and so had not bumped anything. The room seemed to be exactly as when they drifted off.

She gave the curiosity a mental shrug. Since she was

up, they might as well move to the bed, where they could escape what might be the beginning of a kink in the neck for each of them.

Cate put a hand on Lucas's shoulder and shook him gently. "Wake up, time for bed."

She gave him a moment, waiting for him to rise. The day must have been harder on him than he let on; he didn't budge in the least. She shook him again, with more insistence. Still, he did not react, yet his chest continued to rise and fall in its slow rhythmic fashion.

She could feel the panic rising, afraid she might be caught in a nightmare after all. Worse, Lucas might be. She didn't want either of them stuck in one of her awful dreams. In fact, she didn't want to be the object of attention at all. Cate scanned the room, looking for any shining surfaces. Nowhere did she find her reflection peering back at her. Nor did there seem to be any other Cates standing around ready to attack. She breathed deep, forcing herself to relax, easing back into the couch. She put an arm around Lucas's torso, resting her cheek on his shoulder.

"We should probably go to bed."

Lucas's words were exactly what she needed right now. She smiled and nodded in agreement. She sat up and turned to him, her blood cooling. He was still in the same position. Eyes closed, hand supporting his head with almost ridiculous stability. She sat up, her eyes scanning the room once more.

"Who said that?"

"Come on, Cate; wake up." Again, Lucas spoke to her, but it came from somewhere other than his sleeping form.

She got to her feet, the panic swirling, ramping up into a whirlwind of fear around her. She tried to breathe, but anxiety enveloped her. She had no frame of reference to deal with something like this. Was it a coma? Was it another nightmare?

"Cate? Wake up!"

She looked right at him as the voice spoke again. The sound seemed to reach the place Lucas slept; the place where he should have been speaking from. It carried an echo on it, like it traveled further than from his lips to her ears. She turned slowly, noticing as if for the first time, the living room windows that overlooked the city. She did not see the city tonight. Instead, Cate looked out the windows and back into the apartment – a mirrored apartment where Lucas was up, hovering over her unconscious form rather than the other way around. Her focus shifted from the scene in the window to Lucas's unmoving body and back again. She stepped toward the window; more of the apartment becoming visible as she moved closer.

Lucas was frantic. He paced hurriedly, coming close to the window before whirling back to shake her again. He shook her roughly, then withdrew, obviously afraid of hurting her. He got up and grabbed his phone from the table, clicking the screen and then shutting it off and tossing it back on the table, only to check her again and grab the phone once more.

Cate watched with the same fascinated attention she gave her reflection as it struggled to see through the mist from the other side of the bathroom mirror. Horror seemed so far away at this point. She was uncertain how she could've been afraid at all. Not until Lucas felt for a pulse, and then bent an ear close to her mouth, did she actually understand how drastic he perceived the situation to be.

She backed away from the window, turning to the couch where he still sat unmoving on this side of the glass. Sitting down, Cate curled up with him again. It felt strange to her that she knew the real Lucas was somewhere else, yet this body was warm and calm and felt very much like him.

But it's not him; it's an impostor.

Cate ignored the warning from her frantic mind and closed her eyes. She wasn't sure what else to do; sleep felt as far from her as anything else right now. Putting her cheek against him, and letting her eyes roll up a little, she sought the comfort behind her lids.

* * * *

"Cate!"

Her eyes shot open, the sound battering her eardrums.

Instinctively, her limbs sprawled, grasping, across the couch. Her heart raced, anxiety flooding her veins with adrenaline, making her feverish at both ends of the spectrum. Cate couldn't speak – too many synapses fired at once, trying to process all of the new information. She reached out, open and grasping the air above her as she tried to catch her breath.

Lucas stood at the window as she finally managed a strangled cry. Turning back, the phone at his ear already forgotten, he collapsed beside her. She felt his presence before she saw it through blurred vision, his fingers entwined in hers. Her eyes closed, shutting tight to drive out the tears.

"Deep breaths, Cate. In, out. I'm here."

His words were meant to soothe, and she knew they should, but he didn't tell her she was alright. Cate knew she wasn't; Lucas did too. If she could have spoken, she would've asked him to be quiet. All she wanted at this moment was quiet, and for Lucas to hold her until the panic subsided. He didn't need to be a hero; he already was. Her fingers tightened around his as her jaw clenched, making it harder to fill her lungs to capacity. Cate's vision flared and faded with each punch of her heart, expecting her ribs to crack under the force. Desperately, she dug inside her mind for a pleasant thought to hold onto, but her thoughts screamed against the peace.

This is it. This is the end.

But the end didn't come; especially not with the swift certainty her anxiety promised. Life moved on as pain and panic ebbed slow, draining away into the background. Painfully slow. Cate hardly noticed the reduction at first, but the ghostly grip on her chest, a weight that held her breath captive, was suddenly gone. Her pulse and breathing slowed, the thundering in her chest subsided, and vision returned to normal. Tears ran down her cheeks as if to relieve the remaining pressure.

Reaching out, Cate pulled against his grip, using the leverage to help her to a sitting position. Up and seated, she drew him in until her arms wrapped around, squeezing as if her life depended on it. She felt Lucas holding as tightly to her, the warmth of hot tears staining her neck. Cate felt the unsteady rocking of muscles trying to contain the well of emotion as Lucas willed himself steady, his voice unflinching.

"I thought I lost you," the words were almost loud enough to be a whisper, hardly louder than his own breath. To say it any louder would crumble the fragile reassurance that held them together.

"I thought I was lost, too." Over his shoulder, through the tears, Cate was surprised to see the cityscape outside the window. Out there, away from the seriousness of the room, the city glittered, pretending that everything was right in the world.

NINETEEN

"No, I'm telling you: it's *not* in my head."

"And we are telling you, kindly: this is the real world."

Cate covered her face with her hands, growling loudly into her palms. Clearly exhausted, Cate knew the temperamental meltdown of a lifetime was looming. Between the complete depletion of her adrenaline, and the lengthy physical and psychological examination by the paramedics that came at Lucas's call, little sleep was found for Cate. A lengthy discussion had built around what was being called, "the episode." Cate waited in the living room, all but cornered by her closest friends. Mabel, Rachel, and Michael came as soon as they heard and sat around the coffee table, a formidable front against escape to the bedroom. The bathroom was obviously out of the question

— there was no way to barricade it since Lucas last kicked it in. She smiled softly; in any other world, it would have been an incredibly sexy move to behold.

Maybe sometime in the future, when this had all blown over, she would make him kick in another door.

"She's not even listening."

Cate's eyes perked up, proving Rachel right. She had not been listening.

"Sorry, I drifted off."

"To where?" Rachel was working her way down an already short fuse.

"To a happier time, when my friends still believed me and supported me." Her eyes beamed back, daring that fuse to light.

Mabel clapped her hands, flexing her conflict management muscles. "I think that's about enough of the snapping back and forth. It's not helping anyone's case." They all looked at her as if to ask — and then accept — who put her in charge. "Why doesn't everyone take five — go smoke or something."

"But none of us —" Michael tried to interject, but Mabel was already out of patience.

"Or something, then. It's my polite way of telling you to vacate the apartment for a bit."

"What's the impolite way?" Michael's mouth drew up in one corner, a meddlesome glee twinkling behind his eyes.

Mabel looked over her glasses at him.

"Get the hell out of my sight before I ruin that smile, pretty boy."

Michael's smirk evaporated. He looked to Rachel and Lucas, who were already standing, unwilling to call Mabel's bluff. The three of them exchanged looks, then left the apartment without another word. They made no other sound within earshot of the apartment. Where they were going, Cate didn't know, and she didn't necessarily care. Mabel stood at the door waiting, closing it when she knew they had taken her seriously. She paused another minute, a hand pressed against the smooth wood as if to ward off any unwelcome guests for the next five minutes, as directed. From the looks they gave her as they walked out, Cate expected that Mabel had bought herself more time than she requested before they mustered the courage to come back. Mabel returned to the couch, picking a spot close to where Cate was seated. She perched her elbows on her knees, pitching forward as she looked into Cate's eyes.

"This might seem like a stupid question, but how are you, dear?"

She wanted to huff at the idiocy of the question. She gritted her teeth and looked into bespectacled eyes that radiated warmth and concern. Attacking those eyes would shatter everything behind them, and even in her blind aggravation, Cate knew that wasn't the path she wanted to take. She breathed deep, exhaling a hurricane and pulled her hair back. "I am exhausted. Frustrated. I feel alone. No one believes what is happening to me."

"I don't blame you. As metaphysical as Rachel pretends to be, she's not accepting a word of your own supernatural experience."

"Thank you! I wanted to call her a hypocrite, but I knew that wouldn't accomplish anything." She took another breath and exhaled, happy that someone was finally seeing her position.

"Forgive her. She tries so hard to have any sort of experience, and now you have stolen her moment. Even if you didn't mean to."

"She can have it. I don't want it, whatever it is."

Mabel pulled off her glasses, wiping away a smudge that she had accidentally acquired. "And what exactly is *it*?"

Cate stood up, looking out the window, ready to duck for cover if she saw anything she shouldn't. "It's... it's insane. But it's not in my head."

"Explain it to me."

Cate retold the stories that Mabel had already heard. She explained what led up to her hurting her hand, and then wound through her experience with the foggy mirror, and finally landed on the previous night, or "the episode." She expected some sort of wall to come up, or for Mabel to suggest therapy. Instead, her boss – her first friend in the whole city – clasped her hands together in a prayer pose, index fingers pressed to her lips and let one tear roll down her cheek.

"My dear, I wish I knew what was happening to you so I could help you stop it. Unfortunately, I am, like you, completely out of my depth here."

Cate moved forward, kneeling on the floor in front of Mabel's perch and hugged her. "Thank you for at least believing."

"You're a good kid. The only thing that could explain all this is drugs." She grabbed Cate by the shoulders and held her at arm's length. "You're not on drugs, are you?"

"What? No, I —" Cate stopped stammering when the smile snuck across her old friend's mouth. "You are awful. I am being possessed by god knows what and you —"

"What did you say?"

"That you're awful."

"No, after that. Possessed."

"Yeah, I —" Cate watched as Mabel stepped around her and paced, chewing on the earpiece of her glasses.

"No, not you." She snapped the arm of her glasses shut for emphasis. Turning, she tapped the air, making her way back to Cate. "Your mirror."

Cate's eyebrows bunched up as she looked at Mabel, confused for a moment, then the words puzzled themselves into complete sense. Why hadn't she thought of that? It was the only thing that had changed here at home, other than her own turmoil. She had been so wrapped up in her grief and confusion; the mirror was placed and forgotten – how she forgot about the monolith in her own bedroom, she'd never know.

The door to the apartment opened, and Mabel turned, striding toward the small gaggle of people shuffling their feet outside the door. She slid her glasses on and held her hands out, waving them away as if they were self-conscious book browsers who had shown up after she was already shutting the store down. Cate noted that Mabel's authority had already gotten them fifteen minutes.

"Lady, gentlemen, you don't have to go home, but I would appreciate it if you didn't stay here." They gaped, clearly not expecting to be thrown out so soon after they'd returned. "I'll fill you in later – Lucas, you can stay. It is your place." She sighed. "And your girlfriend. But don't think you're not a suspect in this."

She quickly ushered Rachel and Michael out of the apartment, promising to keep them informed on Cate's condition. Lucas barely had time to ask what was going on before she returned like a whirlwind.

"Lucas dear, sit down and hold onto your hat. Also, don't interrupt – it's rude, and I am having a hard-enough time wrapping my brain around this as it is."

TWENTY

They stood in the bedroom, staring at the monolith, quiet and ominous in the corner of the room. The look on Lucas's face was pure disbelief, but he continued to show his support. There was no blame; it would be hard for anyone to buy what they were trying to sell him.

"I'm not saying this is science. I'm not even sure this is superstition, but it's *something*." Mabel chewed on the end of her glasses again. Cate noticed the tic and wondered if it was the reason she changed frames so often.

Mabel wandered around the mirror. She squinted, looking for anything discernible that might set it apart. Her hope was to track the mirror by its history. She looked deep into the lines and curls, attempting to trace an unknown history through its handling. Lucas brought a step stool and a flashlight so she could see over the top arch of the mirror. Unfortunately, there were no specific markings. No signature discerned this mirror from any other like it, which meant no lead on its creator. It was up to Cate and her mother to figure out where the mirror had originated. Or at least where it came from before Harriet acquired it. It was a shot in the dark. They were relying on random and trivial memories; no one else was around who might know the rest of the story. Cate knew Harriet's penchant for auctions and estate sales and crossed her fingers, hoping that something set it apart or this was the end of their search.

Lucas continued to stare dumbfounded as the two women discussed these incidences as if they were commonplace.

"Do you think Harriet's death has anything to do with this mirror?"

Mabel looked at Cate, half-caught unaware. "I hadn't considered that. You said the cause was cardiac arrest, yes?"

"Yes, but in her sleep; peacefully, they said."

"I somehow doubt this thing knows anything about peace. I think it was Harriet's time." She gave the mirror a suspicious glare. "I don't think this thing really understands nuance or subtlety. Covering its tracks would hardly be a thought."

"You're talking about this thing as if it's alive." Lucas finally spoke up, gesturing at the oversized bedroom accent as if they had forgotten what it was. "It's wood and glass. It's not magical. It's elaborate, but it's not possessed. It's a mirror – a fricking heavy one, too."

Mabel's mouth was a thin line as she regarded Lucas.

"I told you that if you were going to speak out of turn, you'd have to wait in the living room."

"I'm not a child, Mabel."

"Perhaps not, but you aren't helping Cate's predicament either. If you are going to naysay everything that is going on here, at least speculate. Pretend it's a game if you must but shut up." She stared coldly at him.

Cate could see they were both tired. She wanted him to help but didn't want him getting in the way of Mabel's brainstorming. His jaw bounced a couple of times and then finally shut.

"Thank you." She turned back to Cate. "If you believe that it wants you, then I doubt it has any intention of killing you. Maybe that's why Harriet never experienced any of this. It's possible it was waiting for someone younger. Stronger."

Tears rimmed Cate's eyes as the reminder of her grief surfaced. It seemed so long ago already, as if so much had happened when it had only been a few days.

"Maybe so. If that's the case, then what do I do? Do I need to develop a terminal disease to be free of this thing?"

"I certainly hope not." Mabel tapped the frame of her glasses against pursed lips as she considered. She turned, tapping the air as her eyes brightened. "Maybe we need to sell it off to someone else."

Cate paused, considering the possibility. "I don't know if I can do that. What if it's not after me specifically? Anywhere this thing goes, it will have someone to hunt. What if it goes to a family? What if it tries to take a child?"

Lucas made a noise, then turned and walked out of the room. Cate winced as if he had said the worst of the things he was thinking. Mabel brushed Cate's shoulder and gave a soft smile.

"Don't trouble yourself with him. He'll come around."

"Are you sure?" Tears still brimmed in Cate's eyes.

"Of course. He loves you. You'd probably be as incredulous if it were the other way around."

"I really don't think I would."

"I know," Mabel smiled, giving Cate's arm a confident squeeze. "But I was trying to give the big oaf the benefit of the doubt."

Cate hugged her. Mabel was like a force of nature; a friendly fairy godmother. Someone able to torture the boyfriend with logic and sarcasm when she was unable.

Cate wiped at her eyes. "What do we do from here?"

Mabel polished her glasses again. "I need to look into some history, and so do you. Talk to your mother. Find out whatever you can. I'll talk to an antique dealer I know; maybe he can dig something up for us."

They turned to walk toward the living room, where

they expected Lucas to be sulking. Instead, his was a face full of worry and apology. Cate was happy to see him at least looking like he cared about what was happening, even if he wasn't going to believe.

Mabel kissed Cate on the temple and gave Lucas a stern look, and then she lit out the door like the fairy godmother Cate thought her to be.

"I'm sorry." Lucas looked like a child scolded.

She paused. She didn't want to give in, but she didn't want it to linger either. "I know. It's okay."

"No, it's not. Something is obviously going on. I should be taking your side, not arguing with you."

She raised her hands. "It's alright. This isn't an everyday couple's argument. It's not like we're debating the color of the bedroom. We're arguing something that shouldn't even be possible."

He stepped slowly toward her, reaching out and grasping her fingers, slowly reeling her in. She let him. Cate didn't care that a part of her was upset. She loved him and wanted there to be peace and comfort while she was being driven mad by ghost or demon or whatever it was.

"I don't know how this is going to end; that's what is killing me." She wrapped her arms around him, resting her head on his chest. "How do I know it's not going to take over and erase me?"

"I won't let it." He held her tight, kissing the top of her head.

"What if you don't know?"

"Oh, I'll know. You better believe I'll know."

"How?"

He pulled away from her, putting one hand on her chest, right over her heart. Lucas grasped her fingers in his other hand, placing her hand over his chest. He let his hand linger over hers until she could feel it glow with warmth. Slowly, he leaned in till their brows met and she could see nothing but his gazing back at her.

"Can you feel that?"

She nodded almost imperceptibly.

"I don't mean my heart."

She nodded again. "I know what you mean."

"Good. *That* is what will tell me. No one else will ever be able to share that with me. Not even someone or something that can impersonate every other aspect of you. *I'll* know."

She leaned in again, closing the small distance that remained between them and kissed him hard with everything she had. She pushed that feeling, that sensation, between the two of them and let it burn brighter.

"You are an ass, but sometimes, you are the most wonderful man I have ever known."

"I love you, too."

TWENTY-ONE

Cate woke and waited for a moment, not opening her eyes, almost afraid to look at anything. It didn't feel like morning, and she was terrified to find herself in another dream – or nightmare. So, she waited, holding on to the darkness and hoping slumber would take her again before she had an opportunity to wake up fully. Consciousness continued to creep in on her, making it harder to keep her eyes shut. She growled inwardly and opened her eyes to the black of night. It may have been an hour, or maybe only a few minutes since she and Lucas crawled into bed. Sleep had not dug its claws in yet.

She lay in bed, staring at what she assumed was the ceiling hovering above her in the darkness. She listened to Lucas's breathing: deep, peaceful, not the slightest hint of interruption. A devious thought crept through her mind, wanting to wake him so she wouldn't be alone in this darkness. But what if she found she was trapped in another reflection, unable to wake him? How would she get back this time?

She flicked off the covers and gently left the bed, honestly trying to let him sleep. The covers continued to rustle in the dark and Sebastian voiced his displeasure of being roused. She reached into the darkness, quietly whispering an apology and giving him a quick scratch on the head before slipping from the room. She walked down the hall to the kitchen, where she found a glass and a carton of milk in the fridge. She drank and listened to the city existing, going on with its night without a single consideration for her well-being. She wondered if the universe would notice if she had been replaced. Then, against her better judgment, she started to wonder what else existed in the world that she wouldn't want to know about.

Had the universe put this plan into motion? And for whose benefit? Was it her life or was she a placeholder for whatever existed behind the mirror? She dumped the rest of the milk into the sink. Her mouth had gone dry and Cate no longer had the stomach for philosophy after that thought.

She wandered the apartment, pacing well-worn paths in the dark. Her feet were feeling better. There was an occasional stab of pain when she stepped wrong, but otherwise, she was back to walking fine after only a day or so. Her arm still ached, but she didn't think she'd have to wear the bandages much longer. It already looked considerably better after Lucas had changed them the night before – then again, everything looked better once you rinsed all of the blood away. Her arm had looked like a crime scene that first day. The pain didn't help matters then, but it too had lessened.

She spent an hour, maybe two, standing in the various rooms of the apartment, pacing slowly back and forth, fighting the thoughts and the doubt and trying to have some confidence that the universe supported her existence over her monster. She was almost ready to accept that insanity was a suitable Plan B to being replaced by something living inside her heirloom mirror.

If Harriet had only known, maybe she could have stopped it. But how? And how can I now?

She pondered the thought, considering the options available to her. How much of a connection did they share at this point? Was there a bond or was it trying to latch on? Could she break the mirror and be done with it? Was it possible, or would that release it, like a genie from a lamp?

Cate didn't know how long she had considered such things, but when she looked at her surroundings again, she was standing before the mirror. She could see it looming tall and foreboding in the darkness. A shudder crept through her with the realization that Cate didn't remember walking here. She didn't like feeling out of control, but didn't give the mirror full credit for the maneuver. Autopilot was a close friend, relying heavily on it when getting around, a few times in recent days. Plenty of bike rides to work had been by muscle memory as she let her thoughts wander. Finding her way unconsciously to her own bedroom was no feat of magic.

She stared into the shadowy portal before her, confident her impostor must originate from somewhere within. Stepping back into a pool of moonlight on the floor, Cate watched the light cast onto the reflection, its eyes still shaded dark and hollow. Growling inwardly at her reflection, she watched it grimace back at her. She didn't like the way it looked, the way it quietly observed her, mimicked her.

Cate grabbed a hairbrush from her dresser and hurled it at the mirror. She hardly processed what she was doing until it was done. Her hands rose to her mouth of their own volition to stifle her surprise. The impact would undoubtedly startle Lucas – worse, it could break the mirror and she would find out exactly what kind of awful things happened from seven years of bad luck

She squeezed her eyes shut and braced herself, but no impact came. Not even a clatter as the brush hit the floor. Peering around in the darkness, looking for the brush, Cate didn't know how she missed the mirror altogether. She stood, silent and uneasy, breathing in and out as she watched her reflection. It was getting to her. It was, whether by design or by Cate's own resistance, changing her. She was on the defensive constantly, nerves taut and fraying. It wasn't a place Cate liked to be. She wanted to be sweet, funny, soft-spoken Cate again. She wanted her life back, with or without her grandmother. She accepted that Harriet's time was over; she refused to accept that her own time was up.

She turned her back on the mirror, walking along the bed, dragging her fingers along the blanket until she heard the familiar purr of a suddenly awoken Sebastian. Brushed her fingers down his spine, his tail twirled as his purring ramped up. She scooped him up into her arms and held him close, nuzzling her cheek against his and kissed him on top of his head.

"Keep me safe, Sebastian." Cate didn't actually know if he could, but he meowed in agreement all the same. She carried him to the head of the bed where she sat down, letting him curl up in her lap. Then with a simple turn onto her side, she cradled the furball close until she fell back to sleep.

TWENTY-TWO

The morning was sullen. The sky was grey and held no hope for improvement. Likewise, Cate woke under a dark cloud of her own with no reason to be positive. Before she was properly awake, Lucas had kissed her on the head and informed her that she was to stay home and relax. It was as if the previous day was all but forgotten. If the mirror is the source of her issues, why would she remain under house arrest with it? Logic had taken a sudden holiday. Mabel considerately refused to let her come in, making one of the part-timers fill in instead. Lucas and Rachel both seemed to agree with Mabel. Even the argument of "seriously, I'd rather be *anywhere* but here" was not working, even though it was true. Why would Cate want to be in the same place as the source of her fears? But Mabel was resolute: she wanted Cate at home, tracking down the mirror's history as best she could.

Cate followed up on her only lead: she called her mom. Her mother, however, was not much help. She could only repeat the vague details given the day Cate discovered the mirror: it was an auction prize sometime after her grandfather passed. Her mother couldn't be more specific.

"To be honest, that thing gave me the creeps any time I was there."

"So, something gives you the creeps, and you think it's okay to pass it along to your only daughter?"

"Your grandmother would have wanted you to have it."

"That's because she didn't realize –" but she couldn't finish. She knew her mother would react worse than anyone. It already sounded insane, meaning it would definitely sound insane to her mother. She already thought Cate exercised too much hyperbole in everyday life.

"Didn't realize what?" The question hung on the line.

"That I wouldn't really have room for it. And you're right; it *is* creepy."

"Well, maybe it will grow on you."

I don't want it to grow on me. I want it gone.

But she didn't say that either. "So, no idea where she got it?"

"She got it from one of those crazy auctions she loved going to with her sewing circle."

"Ah, yes." The sewing circle was a nickname. Harriet's circle didn't sew much more than gossip. Most of her "sewing" circle was comprised of neighborhood widows. Each of the ladies in their group had been a gossip of the highest order.

"Only in friendly ways," Harriet added when telling stories. But if there was a rumor to be spoken, Harriet's circle was a welcome ear.

"Do you happen to remember who ran the auctions?"

There was a chortle on the other end of the line. "As if I'd – wait. You know, I don't recall exactly but," she drew it out, as if she were a game show contestant, "I think it was a pirate's name."

"Like Blackbeard?"

"Don't be silly, I'd remember that. No, it was normal, but I think a pirate name too."

"Alright, well, thanks. I think." She had asked the gods for a favor, and true to Greek pantheon style, they smiled and handed her precisely what she asked for, nothing more. Now, one lead begetting another, she would follow this one as best she could. She paced as her mother caught her up on the rest of the goings-on, the different things happening with the estate and the plans that she had for the rest of Harriet's possessions that hadn't been willed out to family and friends.

But as Cate wandered the house, listening to one story after another, she found herself back in the bedroom, standing before the mirror. Either she had a one-track mind, or her autopilot was caught in some kind of tractor beam. She looked at the reflection, scowling. It scowled back. Then she noticed the hairbrush in the reflection. Somehow it had wound up under the dresser she picked it up from initially. She bent down, reaching under the dresser and padding around with her still-wrapped hand. She pawed as her mother continued to chatter on about how Cate's father didn't understand internet auctions, leaving all the day-to-day work to her. Cate didn't really hear any of it. The words drifted from the phone into her ear, where they rattled around against her eardrum, making a racket. Cate's brain never bothered to process the sounds her mother was sending across the distance. All of her brainpower was caught up in a sudden and challenging game of hide-and-seek.

Putting the phone down, she pressed the speaker button. Her mother's voice was tinny, but loud and clear. Cate stared into the mirror, looking very clearly at a hairbrush underneath the dresser, but felt nothing where her hand searched. Blaming the bandaged hand for her inability, she twisted herself around, face hovering close to the floor. There was nothing under the dresser. No dust bunnies to speak of, and certainly no hairbrush. Twice more, she looked back and forth, unsure of what was happening.

"Mom, I'll call you back later. I've got... something.

Love you." She couldn't even bother with a clever excuse as she disconnected the call.

Looking back to the mirror, she decided upon the impossible.

She focused, watching her reflection's movements. She put her hand out – the good one with the working fingers – reaching to the back to the baseboard. Her hand formed a scoop and dragged forward, out from under the dresser. Her breath caught as she watched the hairbrush catch against her reflection's fingers, dredging out from under the dresser like a lost artifact, or maybe a crappy skill crane.

She stared again, between the floor in the real world and the floor in the reflection. Cate felt nothing – there was nothing – yet moved an object. An object that didn't belong in the reflection; it belonged in her own world.

The mirror had opened and let it slip through. Maybe to reveal itself, or perhaps in self-defense. It was possible that, in some bizarre way, the surface of the mirror had disappeared and let the brush through, to prevent damage done. That meant the mirror was, in fact, a doorway – seemingly one way. It sounded like science fiction: a portal to some other dimensions. But clearly, whatever it was, this was real. Last night, the hairbrush had belonged to Cate, and now it was there with her reflection. Even though the hairbrush no longer existed in her world, she still had control over her reflection and could affect things in that world.

She watched her mirror-self paw at the floor and haphazardly pick up the hairbrush.

Together, they straightened up, kneeling on the floor as they faced one another. They continued their pantomime, Cate raising an imaginary brush to comb through her hair. She watched transfixed as its hair reacted to the object, while hers remained unaffected.

She pretended to brush her hair for a couple more passes and then held her arms out. She stared hard into her reflection's eyes as she raised one arm, dropping it in a sharp movement past the other. Cate's arm followed through, wind whistling around her forearm as the clenched hand passed unimpeded beyond the point of contact. In the mirror, Cate's reflection struck out, smacking herself with the hairbrush. The back of the brush collided, her reflection's arm pressing harder against the point of connection until the handle snapped. The brush fell away in two parts as Cate pushed herself back to her feet and walked to the mirror. She held her arm up to the reflection. In the mirror, she could see a deep red welt forming, but examining her own arm, there was nothing.

She smiled, but she swore she could see anger glittering in her mimic's eyes. Cate had found a loophole; now she had to exploit it. Maybe she could even convince Lucas and Mabel that she wasn't insane. Maybe she could send other things through the mirror as well. If it was possible, she could end this once and for all.

She felt the anxiety slipping away from her. Some of her confidence was returning. There had already been plenty of moments that this mirror had taken away from her. Now, Cate could feel the worry melting away. She was ready to take some of that power back, no longer feeling trapped with the mirror. For once, she was starting to feel more like predator than prey. Maybe she was even gaining the upper hand.

She smirked at her reflection again. Mirror Cate flashed back the exact same look, but this time Cate was certain that there was something else behind it. She sensed more than saw it, but she couldn't decide if it was threatened or threatening.

TWENTY-THREE

Lucas helped Mabel close the shop and together, they returned to the apartment to check on Cate. Lucas had barely slipped his key in the door when it flew open. Cate grabbed him by the arm, pulling him inside, leaving Mabel surprised and suddenly alone in the doorway.

"You need to see this!" The alarming jolt told him panic was the proper response, but violence was not yet necessary as his eyes darted around for clues.

"What happened? Are you okay?" His brain was barely able to keep up with new information being reported as Cate tugged, pulling him toward the hallway while he tried to hold her in place, wanting an explanation.

"Talk to me!" His eyes swung back to the door where Mabel watched the struggle with quiet amusement as Cate dragged him further along the hall.

Cate tugged at him again, and Lucas pulled back. He held her shoulders and wanted to scream. Instead, he clenched his teeth and bit it back.

"Would you tell me what's going on?"

"It's better if you see for yourself."

"I'd rather you explain what we're doing."

She broke from his grip and turned, no longer pulling him along. She left him standing halfway between the living room and the bedroom, marching into the bedroom without another word spoken. Before he had an opportunity to process the change, a whisper crept to his ear.

"Sometimes it's better to go along for the ride." He could almost hear the smile in Mabel's voice as she spoke. She stepped around him, continuing down the hall where she followed Cate's path. When he was sure no one could see, he rolled his eyes and followed slowly.

Lucas rounded the corner to find the two women staring into the mirror. They appeared to be transfixed. Twice Mabel adjusted her glasses, pulling them off to clean them, but the look on her face told everyone that no amount of cleaning would assist with what she was seeing.

He stood in the small gap between them, trying to understand what was so amazing; why they stared so intently. He waited for someone to explain, or maybe give a hint, but they remained silent, occasionally looking at each other and the floor.

"I don't get it."

"Because you're not paying attention." Cate blurted, gesturing at the space ahead of them. He looked at the reflection and saw Cate's over-sized wooden hairbrush. It had been broken and discarded on the floor. It, apparently, was the thing they were both transfixed by.

"I still don't get it."

"Why don't you be a gentleman and collect the pieces for us?" He heard the attitude in Mabel's voice but didn't understand why she was giving it. Maybe if he did what was asked, the spell would be broken. He started to bend, reaching forward –

"What the..."

"Get it now?"

He stood, looking behind them, around them, searching everywhere. He walked around the mirror, looked back at them, and then examined the reflection again. Then he could only stare at Cate; words suddenly failed him. She turned to him, smiling softly. She took his hand, kissing his knuckles as she watched part of his world shatter inside.

"It's okay. Me too."

He stammered, but could not actually form a sentence. She moved him to the side, where he could still see, but she could move between them and bent down. Watching the reflection, she picked up the brush head and ran it through her reflection's hair while they watched her pantomime with practiced efficacy.

The look on Mabel's face told Cate she was caught between wanting to experiment further and wanting a moment to process this new layer of reality.

"Alright," Mabel spoke quietly, almost breathless. "I think we've seen enough for now. Time for tea."

Mabel took Lucas by the wrist, leading the doe-eyed boy out of the room before his brain melted. Cate let the brush clatter soundlessly on the floor in the mirror bedroom. Again, she made eye contact with her reflection, looking for some hidden emotional note behind the eyes. There was nothing this time; plain old Cate stared back through the glass. She turned away from the mirror, ready to see exactly what they both thought now.

* * * *

Mabel set the kettle to boil and returned to the living room. Cate sat next to Lucas, trying to be attentive without a blistering, "I told you so." He was clearly shaken.

"Now you get what I have been dealing with." She took his hands, holding them tight. He squeezed back, looking at her.

"I don't... how?"

She could only shrug. There was no explanation as far as how, only something that was. No how, what, or why;

only where and when. Even those were not complete answers.

Mabel set cups before them, pouring the tea, while they waited for Lucas's world to right itself. She sat across from Cate, unsure where to begin the discussion. They looked at each other for a long time. Cate could see the discomfort in the lines on her usually soft face and took it upon herself to break the silence.

"Mom gave me a couple of ideas, but nothing solid. She doesn't know any better than we do. We're in uncharted territory."

Mabel nodded thoughtfully, taking a sip of her tea. When she looked up, she winked at Cate and smiled.

"Always one to set a precedent, aren't you dear?"

TWENTY-FOUR

Mabel was balancing running a business with worrying about her friend and still calling in favors without raising too many serious questions. It wasn't fair to ask Cate to live down a crazy label, but it would be destructive for a known pillar of the community like Mabel to suddenly develop one. Yet, she was still trying to do what she could for her friends.

Cate, for her part, had managed to run down a lead from her mother's clue. She also gained a bit more insight into her mother than she might have wanted to know right now. The auction house was Morgan & Henries, which her mother associated with Henry Morgan, celebrated buccaneer and even more celebrated liquor mascot. She tried not to read any more into it.

She talked with a seemingly kind, soft-spoken agent named Kevin. She provided him as much information as she could regarding Harriet, the mirror, and all manner of related things. Kevin promised that he would look into the archive and try to track down whatever information he could about the account and its history. She'd receive a call when he exhausted his search, which meant Cate was back to either waiting or bumbling around in the dark.

The problem for Cate, as far as trying to set out a plan, was first, knowing what she was planning for, and second, what she was planning against. Neither was something she could look up, as they had tried – and so far, failed – at every turn related to that task. She collected the knowledge she was able and tried to figure out the rules for herself. With hope and a little luck, the loopholes would present themselves.

She already knew that hers was not the only mirror that was affected. All reflected surfaces seemed to have potential, but she had to be standing in front of one for it to work. If her reflection didn't appear, neither did her mimic. So far, she had only seen it in mirrors – in real life, anyway. In her dreams, dark glass worked as well. For all she knew, any drinking glass could be affected – perhaps even a still enough liquid surface.

Imagine trying to hide from your reflection forever...

Cate tried to shake off the paranoia and focus on what actually happened, not her imagination.

The mirror was some sort of doorway, and at least partly physical. She thought the effect might be for self-preservation, or why didn't her doppelgänger come out already? Was it only a one-way door? It had been dark, but she assumed that the hairbrush had a reflection before she threw it – probably during as well. But when it hit the mirror, it passed through, and the reflection did not cross over.

Maybe her reflection wasn't trying to get out of the mirror. Maybe it was trying to pull her in. If that was the case, she only needed to avoid getting close to it. Well, it and every reflective surface she came across if Cate ever wanted to feel safe again. Her brain returned to cataloging a mental list of anything that could cast a reflection. The list was already exhausting.

No, she couldn't avoid it forever. It would be near impossible. She would have to live like a crazy person. She wasn't sure she could explain to her family and friends why she could only drink liquids in the dark. She wasn't even sure that Lucas would go along with it forever.

Poor Lucas. He hadn't really spoken since he'd witnessed her evidence. She had single-handedly shattered his reality. She hadn't meant to, but at the same time, it was her only option. Cate couldn't live with him thinking she was crazy or lying. If he couldn't handle this, she might be heartbroken, but at least he wasn't misled.

She and Mabel discussed destroying the mirror at

ANDY LOCKWOOD

great length. Hitting it with a hammer, or dropping it out a window, almost comically, into the street like in a cartoon. There was no telling what might happen if they did that. It could end the whole issue – or it could make things worse. What if the power that kept her duplicate in the heirloom mirror dispersed, allowing it to manipulate any mirror at any time – or affect any person it wanted? Cate didn't think she could handle being responsible for letting that evil loose on the world – even if it saved her in the process.

She considered the prospect of throwing something else at it. A brick, maybe. If it didn't break the mirror, then it might pass through to the other side and Cate could use it to bludgeon her reflection. Could she murder her doppelgänger? Time would certainly tell. That was if she could convince herself that the possibility of breaking the mirror would have no real effect on things around her.

She poured herself a glass of wine and considered the options long and hard. In reality, any one was as good as the next. She didn't actually know if any of them would work. There weren't real accounts about haunted mirrors. There were fantasies and folklore regarding *enchanted* mirrors, and a few stories about reflections, but nothing that discussed a separate entity existing within someone's own reflection. All of her research led back to the interpretive understanding that the reflection was how she saw herself – in her dreams or her subconscious. If she saw her mirror self as strange and behaving unusually, all of the books agreed that she believed herself to be strange and unusual. Cate knew better. She knew herself well enough to recognize an impostor on the other side of the glass, and she wanted it gone. When she looked in the mirror, she wanted to see her own smile and her own glittering eyes looking back at her.

She drained the glass and decided that she had to know what was going to happen, one way or another. She went to the cabinet under the kitchen sink, digging out Lucas's toolbox. Flipping the locks open and lifting the hinged lid, the hammer waited for her on top of the interior drawer. Cate closed her fingers around the rubber grip and lifted, feeling the heft of steel. If this didn't do the trick, she wasn't sure what would.

She moved down the hall, fingers flexing in rhythm along the handle as the hammer dangled, swinging slightly. Cate stepped through the doorway and approached the mirror, careful not to get too close. She planned to throw it, so she didn't have to get within arm's reach – she didn't know how it might try to defend itself.

If you're close enough to touch it, it might touch back.

She looked into the mirror one last time, looking for some sort of hesitation or pleading from her mirror-self. She saw nothing but her own reflection dangling a hammer from her hand. She raised the tool, pulling it back over her shoulder and brought her arm forward. Her arm was extended, but her fingers would not let go of the handle.

She looked into the mirror and saw nothing new; her own reflection looking confused and frustrated. She grabbed the head of the hammer in her other hand and easily removed her fingers from the rubber grip. It was as simple as opening her hand. She closed and opened her fingers around the handle a couple more times before raising it again.

A second time, she pulled back and threw her arm forward. A second time, her arm stopped shy of full extension, still holding tightly to the hammer. She stared at the reflection again. This time, it glared back at her, shaking its head. The reflection deftly spun the hammer in its hand, turning the claw outward and pointing the head of the hammer toward itself – toward Cate. Then, with a flick of the wrist, her reflection cracked itself in the head, an inch above the temple with the flat steel head.

Cate would have considered all this to be peculiar behavior for a reflection to have – even hers in recent days – but she was already teetering backward, the floor rushing up at her as she fell unconscious.

Twenty-Five

Lucas's voice came to her from far away. Cate heard him through a murky fog, calling over and over, but she couldn't bring herself to respond. Unconsciously, she drifted closer to his voice, rising through the miasma. In the darkness that encompassed her, she ventured ever closer, even if she couldn't see him. She very much wanted to; there was something important that she needed to tell him.

All at once, sight and sound came back to Cate. Lucas knelt over her, patting her cheek and calling her name. Her eyes fluttered as she tried to open them, trying to respond. He seemed excited and relieved that she was looking at him, his words a blur as her brain processed incoming stimuli slower than she was accustomed to.

What little information got through was obliterated by the blinding pain exploding in her head, searing every last thought in mind. Her hands flew up, holding her head as she bit down on an escaping cry of pain. Immediately, she regretted the gesture, the pressure only making things worse.

Lucas grabbed her hands, putting them on her chest gently. "Easy now, I'm sure that hurts a lot. What the hell were you doing?" He placed a cool cloth on the bright pain above her brow, and a bag of ice on top of that.

She tried to remember, her thoughts lost in a haze of fog and pain. Was she going to do something with the mirror? She let her hands fall to her sides, grasping at nothing.

The hammer.

Where was it? She pawed around, but her fingers kept coming up with fabric. Lucas must have moved her to the bed when he stumbled upon her unconscious form.

"Smash it."

"What?"

He looked confused as he held the compress over her eye. His eyes moved to her hand, limply gesturing at the floor.

"Smash the mirror."

"Cate, relax. You've had another episode. You could have killed yourself."

Her eyes widened under the compress; she could not

believe what she was hearing. The words hurt her more than the hammer ever could; they made her want to cry. He saw the same thing she and Mabel had. They showed him the truth, and now he chose not to believe. It was a complete betrayal. Cate turned her head away; she didn't care if it hurt, she couldn't look at him. He moved the compress to adjust for her repositioning, but he didn't try to force her to move her head back.

"I can't believe you." She forced the words out in a choke; the tears were already coming.

"I couldn't anyway; it's not here anymore." The words sent a shock down her spine. She sat up, ignoring the stabbing pain in her skull as she looked to the now-empty corner of the bedroom.

True to his word, the mirror was gone.

Cate collapsed back into bed against the pillows.

"What have you done?"

"Out of sight, out of mind. You need to get your life back in order. You were obsessed and that mirror was destroying you. Now, it's gone."

"Where?" She turned to look at him, her eyes pleading. She needed to finish what she had started.

Lucas turned away. "Somewhere it can't bother you anymore."

TWENTY-SIX

Two days passed and Cate begrudgingly felt herself returning to normal. She hated admitting that Lucas was right; all but refusing to do so in his presence – but it was true. Without the mirror in the apartment, she could feel herself drifting back toward regular old Cate, where she wanted to be. She confessed to Mabel her first day back: the nightmares had ceased and she was all but living a sane life again. Now the trouble was an overwhelming fear for whoever had the mirror. She tried to pry, but no one would tell her, so instead, she found herself warning anyone that would listen.

Mabel seemed to be the only one who understood.

"If it's not affecting me any longer, that means that it only has power when you are in proximity with it. That means anyone around the mirror is in danger."

"Cate dear, it's alright. Nothing else has happened, I promise. Let yourself forget."

She wanted to take Mabel's advice, but she couldn't; nor would she.

It was tempting to be lulled back into the security of a normal life. One where nothing in particular happened. She had found an uneven stride that used to be her routine and was trying to make it comfortable again. She worried that it might not ever be, but some moments reminded her what she was working for. They were simple victories like a good night's sleep and genuine laughter. Laughing for the sake of laughter was good. She had almost forgotten such things when she was swept up in the maelstrom of the mirror.

Somewhere in the balance between home and work, she found a new stride. It wasn't the same rhythm she was accustomed to, but she was getting there. She still had an aversion to her own reflection – she flinched at the sight of herself unless she was prepared to see it. But the routine was helping; being out and about was helping. Everything was swimming in the right direction until the unknown number came up on her cell phone.

She had left the store to get everyone lunch from King's Deli when her phone started buzzing. She expected it to be Rachel, who had a terrible habit of changing her mind moments before – and sometimes after – the order was in. She stopped on the corner and stared at the strange number.

For a moment, she let it buzz in her hand. It could be a scammer, or maybe a collection agency. Something in her brain insisted that Cate answer the call. She clicked the green button on her screen and raised the phone to her ear.

"Hello?" She spoke, and there was a sudden shuffle on the other end of the line as if the caller hadn't expected a live voice.

"Hello, Cate?" He sounded unsure of himself, and Cate imagined him double-checking the phone number as he stopped speaking. Still, something about him sounded familiar enough to keep her on the line.

"That's me. Who's this?"

"Yes, sorry, this is Kevin from Morgan & Henries, the auction firm. We spoke a week or so ago."

The bottom dropped out of her stomach as she recalled not only the conversation but the dread and fear she had been feeling at the time, how the desperation and the loneliness surrounded her then. Had she let it all go so quickly?

"Hello?" He was hesitant as if the call had disconnected without his knowledge.

"Yes! Sorry, I do remember. It took a moment." She was too exuberant, too loud.

"Not a problem; we all lead busy lives."

"What can I do for you, Kevin?"

"Ah, actually, it's a matter of what I can do for you. I promised to call when I had exhausted my resources."

"It's alright; I didn't hope for much."

"No, you misunderstand. There's quite a mystery surrounding this mirror of yours."

Her pulse quickened. She hadn't actually expected him to indulge her request. She anticipated it all to be niceties, and that would be that without another word. But now, he was not only calling her back, but he had discovered something. She found a bench to sit down at and gave him her full and undivided attention. Lunch would have to wait.

"Go on."

He cleared his throat. "First, I have to warn you, it all sounds pretty crazy."

"It's alright. I'm sitting down."

Her phone beeped, indicating someone else trying to ring in. She ignored it, focusing on Kevin's report.

Kevin had traced the mirror back almost a century, where it had surfaced in New England. No one seemed to have any record of it before then. It appeared to blink into existence in the late 1800s. From there, it worked its way through a handful of owners across the decades, moving back and forth across the country multiple times. He explained that it was an auction house favorite. An item that, because of its enormity and flawless construction, came with a perceived value. It was a guaranteed winner on the auction block, and as it crept back onto the circuit every so often, people were constantly on the lookout for it.

"Why was it sold so many times?"

"That's part of the craziness." He cleared his throat again. "There's a pattern, starting with a vineyard owner in California."

"What happened?"

"He died. He was an older gent. He picked up the mirror from a collector, had it for a few years, then passed away. Everything in the estate was handed down to his children. The mirror went to his son. A couple weeks after he claimed the mirror, he disappeared."

Cate swallowed hard. "Disappeared?"

"He left everything behind. Money, property, family, he gave it all up."

"And no one looked for him?"

"They did! For years. He was never seen again."

"Right, craziness."

"It gets worse." Kevin paused, possibly for dramatic effect, possibly to give Cate time to move to the edge of her seat. Another beep tried to interrupt the silence, but it barely registered as Cate waited with anticipation. "He wasn't the only one."

"Other people from the vineyard?"

"No, his estate sold everything off. The mirror went back on auction and was sold to a couple from Texas; oil money. They had it for a few years as well, until they both passed away. They didn't will it to anyone, so it went back on the market. It keeps bouncing like that: Older people buy it, they die, it goes to someone else, or it goes back to auction. Usually, when it goes back to auction, it's purchased by someone else who is older, who owns it for a few years or so, then they pass away."

"You said it gets worse."

"It does. Sometimes, the owner is new money. Or it's willed to family – usually a child. Of course, when I say child, I mean adult – but they're young."

"That's when it gets worse."

"Right. I don't know how to put this kindly, so I'll spit it out: if you're in possession of the mirror and you're not old, you're going to disappear. It sounds crazy, I know, but that's what I found. They've *all* disappeared; without a trace."

His voice strained as he said it. It wasn't a statement; it was a warning. Cate's pulse thundered in her ears. Wherever the mirror was now, someone was in danger. She was angry, upset, frantic, but she was also breathing a sigh of relief internally. Here was this stranger who owed her nothing, didn't even know anything but her name and her number, but he had single-handedly proven her a still-sane woman trapped in a crazy situation.

"Kevin, thank you so much! I need to hang up, but thank you!"

"Be careful, Cate. That thing is cursed."

"I know. I will. Thank you."

* * * *

Rachel's face shared both relief and confusion as Cate walked back in.

"Oh, thank god, we're – where is the food?"

Cate strode past, barely registering multiple requests for an answer. Her legs scissored in quick, long steps, not bothering to slow down when she hit the door to the office. Mabel jumped in her seat, not expecting anyone to kick down her door and seemed doubly surprised by what must have been a wild-eyed look on Cate's face.

"Did you have trouble getting the order? Rachel tried to call, but –"

"Do you have it?" She interrupted, every fiber in her body knew it was rude and that Mabel tolerated so many more things than deliberate rudeness, but this was no time for games. Audacity was the only way to get her point across.

Mabel stared, likely trying to decide which response she should offer. Cate didn't wait; if it wasn't going to be a direct answer, she had no time for it.

"I need to know if you have it, Mabel. If you have it, then I can put this aside and stop being crazy and accept that there's nothing that can be done." She took a breath, holding up her hand as Mabel opened her mouth, ready to cut in. "But if you don't have it, I need you to tell me where it is. Something horrible is going to happen to whoever has it, and it will be your fault. Yours and Lucas's. I'll feel responsible, but it won't be my fault, because I'm trying to prevent it."

"Cate, drop it. Please."

Cate punched the desk, crying out in frustration. Tears brimmed, running down her cheeks as she shook bodily as if by sheer physical will she could make Mabel understand.

"I know where it came from! I know how this ends! Why can't you see that? Why aren't you listening? It's going to kill someone!"

Even through the haze of hot tears, she could see Mabel trying to hide her guilt. It was all she needed to see. She wanted to scream some more. She wanted to condemn Mabel, and Lucas, and everyone who had betrayed her and made her feel outcast. Cate didn't have the strength to speak her mind any longer. She heaved a sigh, her shoulders quaking with guilt and misery, and shook her head as she walked back through the bookstore and out the front door.

TWENTY-SEVEN

Her outburst should have cost Cate her job, not to mention her friendships. But Mabel and everyone else seemed to be turning the other cheek. Cate didn't know how to react to this. They were making a quiet show of solidarity – a statement that they had forgiven her, but she didn't require forgiveness; she wasn't in the wrong. So, in her own silent statement, Cate refused to speak to any of them unless forced to, for work purposes only. At home, the same rules applied.

She had all but driven the wedge between herself and Lucas. There was a chasm between them and no matter what happened, it wasn't something either of them could get around, no matter how much Cate wanted to put things right between them. Lucas was still withholding information: where it was, who it was with, whether or not it was destroyed. Cate was still obsessed with finding a way to stop it, destroy it, anything she could to prevent it from ruining – or taking – another life. The problem was everyone else only saw her obsession with the mirror, not her need to end its cycle. But she was no longer allowed to talk about such things, so she didn't bother speaking at all.

It wasn't until the third day of her silent protest that she finally had a conversation with Lucas. Neither of them had to work the morning shift – possibly something Mabel had engineered herself. Cate was the first one up, so she started the coffee and got breakfast going. She popped some bread in the toaster and started working on scrambled eggs. It was the sounds and smells that pulled Lucas out of bed, the last one roused – Sebastian had already woken, begging for a taste of any of the delightful smells he was not allowed to have.

"Good morning." It was a reflex; a habit. She wanted to take it back, but really, only part of her still resented him. That was the same part that wanted to hold him down and torture him for the information she needed.

"Good morning." He was groggy, still half-sleepwalking. She slid him a cup of coffee – black with a splash of water to take the edge off – he smiled and took a deep breath with the mug directly under his nose. "Thanks."

"We're out of garlic, and I used the last of the onion."

"Red or yellow?"

"We have yellow?"

"Yeah, in the veggie drawer."

"We don't keep the onions in the veggie drawer," she started and she heard him groan in agreement, opening the fridge.

"Because it makes the rest of the vegetables stink like onions. You're right, sorry." Lucas threw the small fishnet bag from one drawer to the other, closing the refrigerator. Cate tried to suppress a smile as she distributed the eggs onto two plates. He surprised her and slid in, scooping his arms around her waist, pulling her back and kissing her shoulder.

"Please tell me this means you're back. The onions are the first sign of what is surely the edge of total anarchy around here. You're the only order we've ever had."

Cate resisted for another moment, then smiled and nuzzled against him. "It's true."

"That you're back?"

"No, that I'm the only order we've ever had." He pinched her and she yelped, slapping him with the dirty spatula. "You can't compliment a lady and try to retract it. That's bad manners."

"I didn't try to retract it; I tried to caution your ego."

"Mabel would agree with me."

"That doesn't mean it's not ego."

Cate picked up the two plates and strode past him; nose up in the air, trying not to smile as she passed.

The breakfast started a pleasant day of what could optimistically be called "normal." They talked, laughed, and prodded at each other in the adorably offensive way only cute couples could. They went to work and continued the same repertoire until the rest of the people in the bookstore made them stop; sequestering them to separate duties seemed to be the only way to do it. Rachel ran interference at the front counter, keeping Lucas at the front of the store while Cate was dealing with backroom stock and repopulating the shelves.

While she was organizing stock in the backroom, Mabel slipped out from behind her desk. She waited for a few minutes, watching intently before announcing herself.

"It's nice to see you back with us. I was starting to fear we'd lost you for good."

Cate hesitated but didn't turn around. "It's not as bad as everyone thinks. Well, it is, but not that way."

"Cate, we may not understand what you went through, but we could certainly see it. You were slipping away."

She turned, looking at an unusually fragile Mrs. Rogers. Immediately, it softened what might have been a bitter response, but it did not change what she meant to say.

"I may have been out of sorts; I admit that. I may have even been crazed, sure, but Mabel, you saw it! You saw with your own eyes, and so did he." She took a breath; she wasn't interested in crying about this; it was supposed to be water under the bridge. "Something like that doesn't stop because you sent it away. It's going to keep doing what it does, and someone else is going to get hurt. Whatever happens, that's on us now."

"Cate, it's not –"

"Yes. It is. You saw it."

Cate turned away, focusing on the boxes of stock in front of her. She didn't want to be a part of the conversation any longer. She wanted to forget so she could get on with her life without the bitterness that crept in every time she saw her friends: those that let her down when she most needed them.

Cate waited for Mabel to push the issue, but she didn't. Mabel gave the girl's shoulder a soft squeeze and went back to the paperwork that kept them in this happy little family.

TWENTY-EIGHT

Cate took it upon herself to close up shop alone that night. The rest volunteered to stay with, but Cate insisted – she needed to prove it to herself. Lucas had plans to go out for drinks with Michael and some friends; Rachel had a date – likely another that would crash, burn, and its charred, smoking remains would be the discussion throughout tomorrow's workday; being the boss, it was an unspoken rule among underlings that Mabel shouldn't ever have to lock up if it could be helped. She was keeping a roof over their heads and money in the coffers; it wasn't necessary that she do the late shift, too.

The evening passed smoothly and without incident. As the hands on the clock approached closing, she worked her way through the shop, turning down the lights, cashing out, and eventually shutting down the rest of the shop before finally grabbing her things and heading for the door.

Staring back into the store, Cate ran down the list of closing items in her head, trying to make sure she didn't forget anything. It had been such a long week; she hadn't even begun to admit to herself how long it felt.

She nodded to herself and turned in place. One foot led the march forward, but the other stopped cold. Michael was standing outside, looking in at her. Cate gave him a confused smile. Was he looking for Lucas? She gulped, a sudden urgency as she resumed her approach.

Michael didn't react as she moved forward, but before she could get to the door, he turned and started moving down the sidewalk, out of sight of the bookstore windows. Cate turned the lock, pushing the door open.

"Where are you going?" The question rang out, but only street traffic responded. She looked in the direction he'd gone, but she didn't see him. Turning to look the other way, and knowing a prank when she saw one, Cate snuck to the other corner of the shop, waiting at the corner. She jumped out with a yell, but no one was there either.

"You're not funny!" Cate was unimpressed. She didn't know where Michael had run off, or where Lucas was, but she was cooling to the prank.

Standing in front of the store, she crossed her arms over her chest. There was no wind tonight, but there was a sudden chill. Cate didn't like it.

She turned to the bookstore to slip back inside, thinking it might be best to go out the back instead. Usually, that was reserved for days when she wanted to exit quietly, but it added minutes to her time, as she had to wander around the wrong side of the block. She looked back into the store. Michael was already inside the shop.

"How did you –" But the sentence died in her throat. A moment later, she suppressed a cry, covering her mouth with her hands.

It wasn't Michael. Or at least, it wasn't completely Michael. She could see the store through him – *through* the window. The keys in her hand clattered as they fell to the ground.

He was a reflection.

She fought the sudden chill that ran down her spine and stepped closer. He was looking right at her. Dark circles were apparent under his eyes; it was clear that he hadn't been sleeping well. A long moment came and went before she realized he was trying to speak.

"I don't –" she began, but she couldn't finish. She cupped her hand over her mouth as she started to cry. Cate shook her head to communicate that she didn't understand. Michael mouthed more words, but in a hopeless, almost pointless way. His eyes never left her. A nervous energy tingled through her, telling her to run. Turning, her foot kicked the pile of keys on the sidewalk. Cate looked at them, knowing she couldn't leave without locking up. The world might be falling apart, but Cate had responsibilities. She steeled herself and walked up to the door, focusing on the lock and the lock alone. When the bolt slid into place, she pulled out her phone and called Michael, certain that it would go to voicemail. As soon as it did, she disconnected and dialed Lucas. It surprised her, but his did as well. She forced her heart to keep beating; he was out having a good time, of course he was, and probably wondering why Michael wasn't there. She hung up the phone. There would be harsh words later.

Two blocks came and went without ever raising her head to see more than the street beneath her. Cate didn't want to hazard a glance at any reflections. She didn't want to know what they held. But after two blocks, she couldn't hold back the curiosity any longer. She looked into the tinted window of a parked car on the curb.

She was there, looking back at Cate, and Cate was almost positive that it was actually her own reflection. For a moment, it seemed like she was alone, but behind her, over her shoulder, Michael appeared, watching her from her reflection. How was he doing this? Could he travel wherever she was? Where they somehow connected?

Then, a darker thought slipped into her mind: did this mean that the creature was loose? Was it the same one that controlled her reflection? Was there more than one? Did the mirror work as a portal, or an entity? She continued to stare, the questions battering her from all sides until someone came to claim the car, glaring with clear suspicion.

She went home without making eye contact with another reflective surface.

At home, she tried to avoid them, but even in her periphery, she could see Michael everywhere. He never moved, but his eyes always followed her. He was there in every surface, watching, exhausted and miserable.

Her only choice was to turn down the lights and avoid the reflections as she had before. Even alone, Cate felt tired and sad, right along side her absent friend.

When Lucas finally returned home, he found her sitting on the couch, staring into space.

"Everything okay?" He spoke softly, as if elevated tones might send her into hiding. His assumption was mistaken. Her eyes flicked up to him, a fire hiding behind heavy eyelids.

"How's Michael?"

He hesitated. "He wasn't there, but he's fine."

"Has he had the mirror this whole time?"

"How did you –"

She stood up and strode across the room. She grabbed Lucas by the hand and dragged him into the bathroom. They stood facing the mirror with the lights off. She made him look in the same direction and then turned on the lights.

As soon as he saw, he jumped, biting back a cry of surprise, but failed. It started as a yell and bled into a laugh as he turned around, expecting to see Michael behind him. No one stood where Michael should be. The laughter died in a soft whimper. Lucas could only stare, blinking, and then looked to Cate. He could not bring himself to look back at the mirror.

"Look." She stared into his eyes, insistent. She was certain that inside, she was freaking out almost as much as he was. Michael was her friend too, and Cate was not heartless. Lucas could only stare back at her, not wanting to look in either direction.

"I... can't."

"But you need to. For Michael. And for me."

He winced and swallowed hard. His eyes twitched, fearful. Cate counted on the guilt that would not allow him to disappoint her again. He had already betrayed her once, trying to forget what he had already seen the mirror do.

She watched him meet his own gaze first. He was pale, his skin waxy with fear, swallowing hard as he stared at his own reflection. Carefully, his eyes drifted to Cate's, who didn't flinch. She felt so stable for once; so confident in this terrible predicament. Maybe it was because she had already adapted. But she was at the epicenter, shouldn't she be *more* disturbed by what they saw?

Lucas continued to stare at her. She made eye contact one time, then her eyes went back up, between them, to that space he did not want to look into.

Minutes passed. Lucas wiped his palms on his pants,

wringing his hands together as he tried to gather courage. Hesitantly, his focus drifted toward the spot between them, his eyes twitching as if his brain begged him to look away. There, between them stood Michael – at least it looked like Michael. There was something strange about him, other than his lack of corporeal form on the proper side of the mirror. In life, Michael had a sparkle that promised mischief was right around the corner – he was known for it. He was almost perpetually emblazoned with a smile, even the barest hint. It's why the girls flocked to him. He was a constant source of youthful vigor. This Michael, on the wrong side of the glass, didn't smile and didn't twinkle. It was more disconcerting to see Michael's face devoid of happiness than not seeing the body reflecting it. His eyes were sunken, empty. He looked lost and alone and sad. He was still trying to speak, but they couldn't hear anything on this side of the mirror.

Lucas reached out as he stared, grabbing Cate's hand. He held it tight and she felt the tension in him release a little when she squeezed it back.

"I'm so sorry."

His voice was choked. She squeezed his hand harder and tried to smile. The smile faltered as her eyes flicked to the Michael in the mirror, but tried to return when her eyes fell on Lucas again.

Cate's voice was quiet. "I don't think we can help him now. I don't know how."

"Whatever it takes, I'm with you now."
"You better be; I need you."

TWENTY-NINE

Cate stood in the doorway to Michael's apartment, listening to Lucas wander around inside. He called out repeatedly for Michael, but realistically, the apartment wasn't big enough to require more than two calls, the second only if he was purposely ignored. One bedroom and a balcony were the only places Michael could have hidden from them; Cate was already certain he would be in neither place. He was nowhere. His wallet and keys were still inside the apartment. The front door was closed but unlocked – something Michael would not have done intentionally.

Cate stepped slowly into the apartment, looking at the tall canvas draped over the mirror. It stood in the middle of the living room, an obelisk out of place in the modern world. It was obvious that they hadn't wanted to carry it any further, and Michael didn't mind abandoning it in the living room. She wondered if he regretted it now.

She pulled back the canvas slowly, almost expecting to see Michael smashed against the inside surface like a pressed flower. Sadly, there was no sign of him here either. There had been no reflection today; Michael had not appeared and Cate didn't want to think of what that meant. Instead, she could only stare at the mirror and sneer. It had drawn Cate back into its clutches, something Lucas seemed foolishly confident he could prevent. Secretly, Cate understood that this was something she would have to fight on her own.

She looked at it, not bothering to look far enough that she saw her own reflection within. She was perfectly fine remembering herself without soulless eyes and a blank expression.

The mirror looked like it was still in one piece, no worse for wear. They had at least treated it well in transporting. She almost wished they had cracked it somewhere along the way.

"Should we smash it?"

She looked up to see Lucas standing in the doorway. He was staring at it with a mixture of horror and unknowing. She shook her head and looked back at it.

"I don't know. There's no manual for this sort of thing. What if we lose Michael?"

He flinched at the question, pausing, then resolved

himself, stepping closer. "Haven't we already lost him? I can't lose you too."

She nodded. Part of her brain said this was a terrible idea, but she wondered if that wasn't the mirror getting back into her head already.

Lucas wandered out of sight again, returning quickly with a claw hammer. It wasn't the same hammer, but her head started to ache at the memory anyway. He came at it from the front, and she held up a hand. It didn't make sense to go at it from the front; she had already seen a frontal assault fail. But maybe from the back, it couldn't defend itself.

She tapped the back of the mirror, unsure why she wasn't saying it out loud. Maybe she believed that it was alive, and like a sleeping dog, it might jump up and bite them to protect itself. She looked around at all of the reflective surfaces in Michael's apartment. It was already watching; it knew what they were up to.

But, Cate wondered, *can it do anything about it?*

Lucas came to the back of the mirror, looking, and shrugged. She peered around the side and understood: the back of the mirror was solid wood, the glass contained within. They would have to pry the back off the mirror to get at the glass within if they wanted to try smashing it.

"Does he have a pry bar? Or an ax?"

He twirled the hammer. "He has this, and a screwdriver. Not even a pair of them. One."

"Philips?"

"Flathead."

"Grab it."

Using it as a wedge, Lucas hammered it into a crease, watching the blade skip along the edge, but never sinking in. Whether age or its own grand design, the wood was no longer ordinary lumber. It had become one solid piece around this mirror, a protective sentry around a portal – the whys and hows still dormant, but starting to eat away at Cate's nagging mind. Lucas worked his way down one full length of the mirror, then shrugged his shoulders in defeat.

"It's petrified or something."

Cate stood in front of the mirror, her reflection sending the hateful look that burned from her eyes right back at her.

"If you want me so bad, come and get me. I'm right here!"

Lucas poked his head out from behind the mirror and waved, trying to flag her off challenging it – something neither of them understood – but it was too late. There was a fire burning inside Cate that threatened to consume her entirely if she didn't put the energy to some use.

"You think I won't come in there after you? Try me."

Her reflection never changed. The blank eyes never appeared. It was Cate, the one and only, posturing back at herself. Tears threatened as she screamed at the mirror, for once wanting to see that humorless soul behind the glass. She didn't want to watch herself fall apart anymore.

Lucas came out from behind the mirror and held her. He put his arms around her and shuttered her from her rage momentarily. His arms quaked around her as she realized, maybe for the first time, that he was utterly out of his depth. He wasn't sure what to do but follow her on this damned crusade. She was certain without even asking, that his plan didn't go much beyond keeping the mirror and Cate apart from one another.

"Maybe I should take you home. You need some rest. We can tackle this later." He nuzzled the top of her head, speaking into her hair. When she didn't respond, he bent his face to hers, to confirm his words were reaching her. Instead, her tear-streaked eyes focused on the mirror. He turned and again, the mirror had the jump on them. It wasn't Cate's reflection she was staring down – but it wasn't Michael greeting them, either. It was Lucas.

It turned the same way he did, matching him exactly. He bristled and it bristled with him. Cate was certain that if they inspected carefully, its hairs would be standing on end as well. Except the duplicate's face reflected nothing of the horror held in Lucas's eyes.

It was only a moment; Cate looked from Lucas to his reflection and back. Perhaps if he had let the impulse travel all the way to his brain and back again, things might have gone differently. Maybe if he had communicated, she could have worked a plan out with him. Instead, he let the impulse become an action without any consideration between the two of them. His muscle groups tightened, following suit all the way up his arm; one set contracted after another until his arm was a coiled tail ready to lash out. Cate didn't have time to react; she was barely able to acknowledge what she saw, much less able to do anything about it. Her eyes grew wide, but the rest of her body was slow to react further.

Lucas, however, seemed poised for action. His muscles contracted and a moment later reversed, pulling momentum, inertia, and the frustration of being trapped in this terrible unknown. His arm extended and his fingers relaxed, letting the hammer curl away from them, hurtling toward its destination. It barely had time to complete a full rotation before inexplicably passing through the surface of the mirror.

Though the world had slowed down enough for them to take in all that was happening with the utmost clarity, Lucas and Cate were still bound to the mortal laws of physics.

In hindsight, Cate could imagine how it appeared to Lucas, having had the same thing happen to her. He would have seen what was coming but would have been able to do frighteningly little about it. He would know in an instant that a mistake had been made, and though a thousand impulses would flash through his brain, he'd be able to execute precisely none of them. He would watch his offense become his reflection's defense, and would come to terms with it in painfully slow resolve.

For Cate, it happened much faster. The hammer seemed to deflect off the mirror, the room echoing with a sharp crack as it connected with Lucas's skull. He collapsed in a heap an instant later, unconscious, and quite possibly in worse shape than he appeared. All she could do was cry out, holding him as she fumbled with the touchpad on her phone for help.

She was wholly oblivious to the two bodies in the reflection watching over the entire ordeal, not bothering to play their own equal and opposite parts on their side of the glass.

Fortunately for Lucas, someone had been there when he had his "episode." Unfortunately, Cate couldn't tell anyone the truth about what had happened to him, so she concocted a story about Lucas playing handyman and accidentally leaving the hammer up on a ledge after he'd put the ladder away. He'd had the brilliant idea to jump up and grab the handle, where he failed to make the catch, and rendered himself unconscious. As much of a stretch as it sounded to her, the EMTs nodded politely. It wasn't the first time they had come across anything like this, and they were certain it wouldn't be the last.

Cate watched them load her precious cargo into the ambulance and then started back toward their apartment, albeit as briskly as she could. There, she gathered a few staples – for Lucas and for herself – and hailed a cab to the hospital.

THIRTY

It took longer to find Lucas than she expected it to. The lobby attendant didn't have any new arrivals listed in her itinerary. This meant that Lucas hadn't officially been admitted yet, or they were lax on updating the digital records. Either way, with no official record, Cate was denied a visitor's pass – and had no idea where to go, anyway.

She clenched her teeth and forced herself to smile. She didn't like the rules, but they were in place for a reason. There was no leverage to force the issue, anyway, so, Cate smiled and asked if she could be pointed to the bathroom. The bathroom, as luck would have it, was much closer to the stairs than she anticipated.

* * * *

After wandering up and down the varied staircases and a couple of wrong turns, Cate found her way to intensive care, where she was certain Lucas would wind up. The nurse's station was easier to find, but she discovered that it was unattended. She sighed deeply, trying to remind herself that nurses had rounds to complete and that someone should be along within a few minutes. Waiting while listening for footsteps in the hall, Cate deciding that all hospitals must be creepier for having night descend upon them. That lone factor separated a busy, populated wing from these empty hallways.

"Can I help you?"

Cate almost screamed; she definitely jumped. Her hands were shaking a little as she smiled, trying to laugh it off as she turned around. The girl behind her looked as spooked and sheepish as Cate herself felt. Her posture was rigid and uneasy, slow to relax while Cate stood there. Part of it was guilt for scaring Cate, but there was something else...

"I am so sorry. I should have realized –"

Cate waved it off. "No, it's alright; I'm a little on edge tonight."

The nurse nodded, pushing her hair back over one ear. "Spend some time on the overnights. It'll make a wreck out of anyone."

"That's sort of the plan tonight. I'm actually looking for my boyfriend."

"Patient or staff?" Without a word further, she moved to the computer behind the desk, clicked a couple of keys and brought the screen to life.

"Patient. He came in a little bit ago."

The girl looked up, her eyes brightening. "MC Hammer?"

"I'm sorry?"

Immediately, the nurse's eyes widened and she shut down. "I am so sorry – again, even. I shouldn't have said that. We had a patient come in unconscious with a blow to the head from a hammer."

"That's Lucas."

If she could shrink down any further, she might have. "I'm really sorry. I give them all nicknames to keep them straight in my head until I have a chance to get to know them better." Her eyes pleaded for understanding, and if circumstances were different, maybe Cate would have laughed long and loud with the nurse. Maybe there could still be time to laugh about it later.

"No, it's fine. Now I have something to call him when he wakes up." Cate forced a smile and the nurse seemed to brighten a bit. "Can you tell me what room he's in?"

A few more clicks on the keyboard and the nurse was back on her feet, leaning across the desk with a dog-eared laminated map between them.

"Room 208. Head back to the stairs – or the elevator – and when you come out on the second floor, make a left. It'll be directly ahead of you, end of the hall." She circled the room with a dry erase marker. "For what it's worth, his chart says he's still unconscious, but he's stable."

Cate stepped back, her feet already turning before she had properly ended their conversation. "Thanks very much, nurse…"

"It's Danielle. I'll be around all night if you need anything."

Cate smiled, nodding as she moved to the stairs rather than wait for an elevator. It took her no time at all to find room 208, exactly where Danielle told her it would be. She pushed the door and was surprised to feel the door resist the opportunity to do its job. She pushed harder, almost expecting to hear the scrape of metal or stone against one or the other, but there was no sound at all. The door, whose purpose was mostly to remain closed so patients of the hospital could rest, begrudgingly opened far enough for her to enter, slipping closed the moment she stopped giving it her full attention.

Lucas lay on the bed, a monitor pulsing silently beside him. Butterfly sutures held the wound on his forehead, though nothing but time would reduce the size of the swollen mass that throbbed over his eye where the hammer had caught him. Instinctively, she reached up, touching her own ghostly bruise. The mirror had been kinder to her. It was trying to teach her a lesson; it was apparently trying to rid itself of Lucas completely. Her jaw tightened, and she wanted to cry, but she held it in and pushed it back down. She didn't want to wake him with her tears.

Cate stared at him, deep purple circles under his eyes, matching the ugly splotch of color on his forehead. She was almost glad that he was unconscious; it would give the pain time to recede. She could only imagine how much more it would hurt if he woke up now.

She pulled a chair closer to the bed and sat down, trying not to stare but finding herself transfixed, comparing the Lucas that lay unconscious in the bed before her to the one she had seen earlier today. It wasn't that she didn't – or couldn't – recognize him, but with his wounds and bruises, she might have mistaken him for a surprise brother or – she suppressed a shudder – an impostor rather than the boy she fell in love with.

She opened the bag she'd brought along and set out a change of clothes and his travel kit. At some point, he would appreciate having the items. Then she sat back and tried to start into the book she had brought along.

The pages turned, and her eyes tracked the words, but there was no comprehension behind her eyes. Cate sat quietly, pretending to read, following the path of the story, hoping to distract herself from both the pain and fear of Lucas's present and future and the dreaded knowledge that she was going back to Michael's tonight.

Somewhere in her brain, she knew it was not only risky; it was probably suicide. They had challenged whatever being was behind the glass and, so far, everyone she knew had come out on the losing side. Michael was gone, probably dead, and Lucas was in the hospital. If she kept on this path, Rachel and Mabel would follow. Cate wasn't sure she could live with the guilt of losing everyone in her life. She set the book down next to Lucas and got up. She moved around the bed, kissing him tenderly on the unharmed side of his forehead and slipped out of the room quietly.

Downstairs, she found her way back to the nurse's station and found herself utterly alone again. She took a questionnaire from the counter and flipped it over to the blank side, writing quickly, hoping her handwriting would not appear too urgent when Lucas finally had a chance to read it. She folded in half, already headed back to the stairs when the Danielle came back around the corner with a smile.

"Something I can help you with?" She skipped a little, trying to close the distance between herself and the girl who looked like she was in a rush to be someplace else.

Cate was suddenly sheepish, self-conscious. She was mentally reviewing the letter for any hints of craziness before handing it over to a stranger, albeit a friendly one.

"There's something I need to deal with. Urgently. If he wakes up before I get back, can you give this to him?

Please?" She held out the folded page as casually as she could, as if handling it too carefully would clue Danielle off to the nature of the message. For her part, the nurse didn't seem to notice and smiled, taking the note in hand and walking back to the desk, where she folded the letter once more herself and slipped it into an envelope.

"Safe keeping." She said it with a smile, writing the room number across the front. Cate felt a glow in her chest for this kindness and wanted to express more than brief thanks. However, urgency tugged at her again, so she turned, running toward the front of the hospital.

THIRTY-ONE

Cate stood outside Michael's apartment, wringing her hands, willing them to stop trembling. The landlord gave her a small wave as she passed through without so much as a question, which might have actually been preferred. Cate would have liked him at least attempting to walk up with her in Michael's sudden absence, rather than leave her to return to the scene of the crime alone.

It *was* a crime, wasn't it? Or was it an act of self-defense? Cate held her face in her hands, fingers trailing down the wrinkles of confusion and worry that had come on so suddenly since her grandmother had passed away. Things had gone so quickly from ordinary to sad to whatever this had become.

Madness. Pure, inexplicable madness.

She reached out, feeling her fingers involuntarily tap out a rhythm on the door handle. Irritation made her grab the handle firmly, perhaps too tightly, and twist the knob. It popped open, continuing to swing free as she released it, slowing and stopping when the door was almost completely open.

The mirror stood, silhouetted against the open windows, the lights of the city streaming through the glass. For a moment, she almost believed it was facing the door, waiting for her. She shook off the ridiculous notion and flicked on the light, stepping into the apartment.

In the space of one step, everything in the room changed. Not physically, but the mood of the room and everything within it suddenly perked up and took notice. If the mirror had been a living person, it would have raised its head the moment she stepped through the door, but it wouldn't bother turning to acknowledge her. It wanted her to make the first move, and she was ready to do exactly that.

Cate took in a deep breath and cleared her mind. She was on a mission, one that no one else needed to be involved in. This was, for some reason, down to her and it. One of them would win this contest, and Cate knew that this torment would only be passed along to someone else if she didn't come out on top.

But how do you win out when you don't know what you're up against?

She shook the doubt from her head and strode into the room. Her heels clicked along the floor as she came around the mirror and spun, ready for whatever it was going to try next.

And for everything she thought she should brace herself for, she hadn't expected what she found.

Cate stared into the mirror, but there was no one staring back. It was more like a doorway into another room – an empty room – than a reflection. She stepped closer, looking back and forth trying to figure out where her reflection had gone, and why her double picked now to abandon her. Reaching out, she tapped the glass. It rang with a hollow reverberation, verifying that the portal was still closed. Part of her was disappointed, but at least it meant that her doppelgänger was still in there somewhere.

Though a small, still-logical part of her brain warned her that it could be a trap, Cate found that she was hovering closer to the mirror's surface.

She wasn't even sure she should call it a mirror now. It was more like a threshold separating this place from that one. A place that looked deceptively real, despite the fact that this was a doorway standing in the middle of the living room. The doorway did not empty into the other half of the living room, but to someplace different – that looked almost exactly the same. She peered in, swaying back and forth in a hypnotizing little dance as she tried to get a good look at what was on the other side of the mirror.

As she stepped closer, her toes stabbed something, pushing it along the floor. She looked down to see the hammer and picked it up carefully in both hands. She didn't think anything could hurt her if her reflection wasn't even here, but there was no point in taking chances. Cate turned the hammer over in her hands; a dirty brown semi-circle marred the otherwise polished face. She swallowed hard, knowing it was blood. A flick of her wrist later, the handle had spun, the ugly reminder turning away from her.

She was ready to set it down when she realized the hammer, though very real, was not Michael's. This hammer didn't belong on *this* side of the glass. The evidence was well worn and almost unseen, but clear in the reflection of the city lights was the manufacturer's logo – backward.

She stepped closer to the mirror and looked around again. It appeared to be as any reflection: an exact but mirror-opposite version of the real world. She could see a book on the coffee table, its print backward on the spine as she looked across the reflected room at it. She stared at the backward book for a long time, her eyes flicking here and there, expecting at some moment for her mirror self to come rushing back in at her, but no one showed.

The longer Cate stared, the more she wondered if she could slip in and take something out again. Her brush had passed through, and the hammer had not only gone through but spit out a replacement. Could she pull something out of the mirror to compare to its real-life counterpart?

She focused on the book. It would certainly provide a compelling argument and give them something to look closer at. But how was she going to get it? She had to cross the boundary not once, but twice to get back. Cate closed her eyes and shook off the fear.

No backing down now.

Cate let the hammer drop and closed her eyes. She took in a long, slow breath and held it. She held it until she could feel her heart slow, then exhaled. She continued until she could feel herself on the verge of drifting to sleep and knew instinctively that she was relaxed – this was the moment.

Cate stretched her arm out into the vacuum before her. With her eyes closed, the world around her felt like a vast emptiness. The sounds of the city seemed far away, out of touch. Her senses, desperate for some kind of input, grabbed at the small sounds – the hum of the light above her, the air leaking through worn seals in the windows – as if they were the most important things in the world at this moment. She turned her mind back to the task at hand and reached forward, her fingers twitching in anticipation.

Her brow creased with frustration. Cate wanted nothing more at this moment than to rush, to hurry, pushing her way through. She knew it would only result in another failed attempt at bringing an end to all of this. She didn't know if there would be an opportunity for a second attempt; she had to get it right on the first try.

Her brain dared her to open her eyes, to see how much progress she'd made. She didn't have to chastise herself for the thought, though she wanted to. She knew better than to look; the fact seemed as crucial as moving slowly and patiently. If she rushed, if she peeked, the spell would be broken. She was certain.

Her fingers crept forward, feeling a change in the temperature around them. Her breath caught in her throat and she had to consciously force herself into a state of calm.

Small air currents danced between her shaking fingertips and the object before her. Cate was trembling. She tried to calm herself, but her nerve was slipping. Part of her was afraid to touch the mirror; another part of her feared something touching her first.

Sparks traced paths up her arm as her fingernails barely grazed the surface. The touch was so light she couldn't tell if she made contact with the solid glass or brushed against something else entirely. She pressed forward, her fingers bending against the resistance of the smooth surface. She pushed until her palm rested flat and a dull pain radiated in her wrist from the force she was putting behind it.

She felt the corners of her mouth turn downward before she ever saw anything. She sighed, her shoulders sloping as she exhaled. She opened her eyes.

Instinctively, she flinched, not wanting to see her reflection gloating back at her before it sucked her into whatever hell it resided in. Cate let her eyes turn back to see her hand firmly placed against the mirror, the apartment mirrored back at her, but her reflection was still nowhere to be seen.

Her knees buckled and she crumpled on the floor. She wanted nothing more now than to push it over, shatter it, and be done with it. She wanted to believe it was ridiculous for an inanimate object to display petty emotions – or emotions at all – but she could almost feel it mocking her, her own emotions boiling over as hot tears flooded her eyes, cascading down her face. She picked up the hammer, screaming, and brought it down in an arc in front of her, connecting firmly with the floor.

Through her misty eyes, it was almost impossible to understand what had happened, but it felt like she had missed the mirror. She wiped at her eyes, looking around. She found herself halfway between the two worlds. The hammer made an awful dent in the floor of the mirror world's reality; most of her body

still kneeling in the real world. She didn't take time to consider how or why this approach worked best. Cate clambered to her feet, holding the inside of the frame like a porthole.

She stepped through and raced for the book. She picked it up and flipped through it, finding that the pages inside were blank, every one of them. She turned back to the mirror and froze, confident that whatever thought this world might have resembled, her guess was entirely off the mark.

On this side of the mirror, there was an inner edge to the frame where it met the glass and held it in place. There was a floor and various artifacts reflected from the real world like cast light. Everything else was blackness. In the space where the light of Michael's apartment did not fall, nothing existed. Where the rest of his apartment should have existed behind the mirror, there was only an emptiness that frightened Cate to her core. She scrambled forward, the book held tightly to her chest as she ran toward the opening, hitting it with the full force of her inertia and bouncing off, scrambling back from the mirror as if the mirror itself had lashed out at her.

"No! No, no, no! I can't –" But the rest of her words were taken from her. Her lips closed as she righted herself, not sure what she was doing as it was not her will. As if caught in a waking nightmare, she stepped closer to the mirror, her stomach sinking as the last bit of warmth fled her soul. In front of her, on the other side of the mirror, was her reflection. Except it was no longer following her. Cate was the puppet now, following every motion that her copy made. It smiled, turning and posing, making quite a show. Cate could only go along – she had no choice. Her body did what her duplicate required; Cate could only scream inwardly. She couldn't even cry. She was certain that a glow of defiance appeared in her eyes. She was aware of how ironic this was; she was now walking the first mile in her reflection's shoes. She understood how it felt first hand: Her reflection couldn't do anything then, and she was unable to do anything now.

It blew a kiss at her, and she blew one back, then strode away from the mirror. Cate matched movements with every tic of muscle until she was out of the reflection. The moment she was beyond the frame of the mirror, her faculties were returned to her. She turned and moved back to the mirror, watching the world on her side of the glass vanish as the lights went off in Michael's apartment. She reached out, grasping for anything that had been there: the book, the table it rested on, the entire living room. It all vanished with the light.

She collapsed, slowly crawling as she moved to the faint image of the dark apartment. She pressed her fingers against the mirror. To Cate, it still felt like a smooth glass surface, but there was another property to it now, something she couldn't explain and probably had no right trying to. When she tapped her knuckles against it, there was no sound, no vibration. On this side, it was more than glass. It was a prison.

THIRTY-TWO

Lucas woke to the sound of someone moving around the bed, prodding gently at him. He shuffled away from the intrusion, noticing almost immediately the rough plastic crinkle beneath him as he adjusted his weight. His brow creased in curiosity, then crumpled under pain of consciousness. In waking, he'd also revived the pain in his head and it wanted to make sure he was aware of the fact.

He let out a groan, and a hand rested upon his.

"Good morning. I'll get you something for that aching head." It was a stranger's voice. He squeezed his temples between the heels of his hands, trying to minimize the ache enough to open his eyes. He squinted through them enough to see a blur of blue scrubs leaving the room. Lucas's eyes scanned the rest of his surroundings, recognizing it as a hospital room.

"How the hell —" He croaked, then bit off the rest of the statement, clenching his teeth against a swell of pain.

"You came in yesterday, unconscious from a head wound." The blonde rounded the bed, proffering a cup of water and a paper shot glass with two large pills. "It's surprisingly common: household accidents. These will help with the throbbing."

Lucas took the pills, guzzling the water. It not only promised to help with the pain but remedied his dry throat as well. The words seemed to strike a chord, some meaning that his brain understood, but was lost to the angry pulse that blocked a majority of his thoughts.

"Thank you, um, nurse?"

She smiled. "Casey."

He passed both cups back to Casey. "Is my girlfriend here? Could you find her for me?"

"She isn't, actually. She was here last night to sit with you, and then she had to leave." She reached out to the bedside table and retrieved an envelope, holding it out to him. "She left this for you."

Lucas tore open the end of the envelope, pulling out the letter. He scanned it, then reread it. He flipped it over to make sure he hadn't missed some crucial part of the message. He was hoping for a "just kidding" or "April Fools," but there was nothing of the sort. She was, apparently, serious.

"Can you get me my phone?" He looked at her, tension rising with every millisecond she hesitated.

"You weren't admitted with one."

"Then I need to get out of here."

Her body language went rigid. "You need to be discharged by a doctor before you can leave."

He stared at her. "Casey, it's very important that you get the doctor so I can leave."

He held her gaze until he could see how uncomfortable she was in this staring contest, but he would not back down; it was too important. He was desperate and if her feeling that helped his case, she would feel it in waves.

"Stay here; I'll get him."

She backed out of the room, turning on her heel to run down the hall. Lucas waited, looking at the folded piece of paper in his hands. Ink and pressed pulp, he tried to tell himself. Characters that joined to make words, words that strung together into sentences. He stopped before he considered the meaning found in those sentences. There should be nothing to fear, but he knew better. Cate had a head start, and she had been up to who-knows-what the entire time he'd been out.

He laughed, but it was not light and joyful. It was bitter, bright with anger and fear. He knew exactly what she'd been up to, she'd told him as much.

I'm going to end it. That's what she'd said. Which meant, more or less, that she went into that apartment by herself, alone with that mirror.

Her and that *thing*, he corrected.

He leaned forward in his bed, feeling his head swim. The pain was receding, but his head was a fog now. He reached out, pulling his shirt off the nearby chair, almost falling out of the bed in the process.

Even if she is still okay, how are you going to help? It was a good question, but he brushed it off. Logic had no place in a desperate man's mind.

THIRTY-THREE

Cate wasn't sure how much time had passed while she sat there, staring out into the vast darkness before her. Time passes differently when there is nothing to calculate by, but she was pretty sure that morning hadn't come. She was almost certain that she'd see sunlight through the mirror when it arrived. In the meantime, though, she had no idea where she was, or how far the darkness expanded. Panic had ebbed, but desperation had settled in thick, leaving Cate to cling to what remained of her window to reality, hopeful that a solution would present itself.

While it initially occurred to her that searching for an alternate exit might prove fruitful, she hesitated, reminding herself that taking on the mirror alone had also seemed like a solid plan. So, she stayed close by, staring into the dark, trying to make sure that there was still a world on the other side. She held onto hope that the portal had to exist as long as the mirror did.

Cate tried to quiet the thoughts racing in her brain, but it was already too late. Like bats nestled into a huddle, once one took flight, it quickly became a jumbled mass of flitting confusion. Perhaps if she were amid the chaos, it might look more like an elegant dance, poetry in motion, but she was in the middle of a black nothing. Not elegant or poetic, nothing.

She wondered if this was what happened to Michael.

In an instant, she was on her feet, feeling like the most selfish person on the planet. Why had she not thought of him already? Could he still be here?

"Michael?" She called out, again and again, hearing her voice swallowed up by the inky black that surrounded her. Distance was as impossible to gauge in her confines as time. If he was here, she didn't know how to begin to look for him, or how to tell if he could even hear her.

Cate took a step away from the mirror and hesitated, how would she find her way back? What would happen to her if she couldn't? She put a hand on the mirror – it was the only word she had for it, even though she knew it wasn't accurate on this side. Here, it was a thin plane hovering in place. She could trace her hands over every inch of it; nothing supported it, yet it stayed in a fixed place, attached to nothing. She could walk all the way around it, though in the dark, she had no idea if there was anything to see from the other side. Part of her doubted that anything was even there, much like the reverse side of any mirror.

Again, she took a step away from the surface. She couldn't sit here, wasting away while she waited for a miracle. Cate took two more steps in what she hoped was a straight line, looking back over her shoulder at a place in the darkness she was almost certain was the mirror. Two more steps, though it didn't feel like she had moved at all.

She was about to take another step when her peripheral vision lit up. She shielded her eyes against the glowing rectangle and imagined her last moments before being run down by a train in the darkness. Her eyes began to adjust as the light persisted without movement or variation. It was a dim light after all, not as brilliant as she first thought. Cate approached the new shape, taking a quick glance at her original portal to keep her bearings. Her eyes lit with pain, forcing her to squint until they adjusted, realizing with trepidation that the darkness around her was so absolute that this small amount of light seemed like overkill.

As if to compensate, she found she could make out details where her eyes shouldn't have been able to. Familiar shapes revealed themselves as recognizable décor. It didn't take long to realize that she was peering into her own bathroom, light tracking into the room from the hall. Cate sighed; she hadn't been trapped as long as she thought – only long enough that her reflection could travel from Michael's apartment back to her own.

Rubbing at her eyes, she tried to understand why this window had suddenly appeared. Her hands snapped to her sides; control of her own body suddenly lost. A shadowy figure emerged from the doorway, and Cate knew it was her. She would have known, even if she hadn't started matching the movement of the silhouette. In the dim light cast from the hall, it was hard not to recognize her own shape. She recognized the otherwise unremarkable differences, too. There was a slight hitch in her reflection's gait, as if she had trouble shifting her weight as she walked. No one else would notice it, but the real Cate did. She wondered if her copycat was aware of it too.

The other Cate was wearing something new – had she come home to change? Where was she going now? They stepped closer to each other, a thin otherworldly veil the only thing separating one from the other, yet worlds away. It took Cate a moment to realize that she was wearing a nightgown. She wanted to shake her fists, to scream, but she could only smile back at her cruel reflection as they admired each other, twisting and turning in front of the mirror in the thin fabric.

Was she going to seduce Lucas? Was she laying a trap?

It was almost as if they were sharing thoughts as well because the other Cate shrugged her shoulders and walked out of the room. Cate regained her faculties and watched the dark bathroom for another minute until the light from the hall flicked off. The bathroom portal faded, even as Cate pressed her hands against it.

She worried about Lucas, and about herself. She tried to wrap her arms around herself; her body seemed less tangible in the darkness. She had limbs, but could barely feel them, as if they lacked substance. Would she stay this way forever, waiting for opportunities to appear as her reflection had? Or would she eventually slip away, leaving no reflection at all? She shuddered – at least she felt she should – at the idea of ceasing to be, blinking out. She didn't want it to end this way.

Cate wandered the darkness, looking for something other than the dark itself. She hoped that daylight would make things easier, but she wasn't sure it would. Reflections were as temperamental in the daytime as they were at night and even if she did get an opportunity, what could she do? She was a reflection here. She had to obey her real-world counterpart.

Or did she? She remembered the moments when she separated from her reflection – when it couldn't follow her exactly. There were moments when it broke away from her. There had to be a way to do it. She would have to stay alert; such an opportunity wouldn't last.

THIRTY-FOUR

The first indication that night was ending came from the old mirror itself. Regardless of how much she thought she wandered, she hadn't drifted far. Maybe it only felt like she was walking; perhaps there was less of her in the darkness than she realized. Although here, standing in the light falling through the mirror's frame, she could see her limbs – and the nightgown the other Cate had been wearing.

She pressed against the mirror, feeling the smooth surface of the glass. She pushed harder, hoping to force it out of the way, but it had no intention of moving.

Over her shoulder, another pane lit up. This one was narrow and similar to the shape of her bathroom mirror. Cate barely had a moment to confirm it as the same bathroom mirror before her reflection hung a towel over the window between their worlds. The portal remained, but it was obscured, hardly visible. Cate had no idea if Lucas had come home. And if he had…

She struck the thought from her brain; she didn't want her only hope to be tainted. It was more likely than not that Lucas had remained at the hospital. He probably hadn't even seen her note yet.

Cate in front of the portal, waiting or an opportunity to present itself. None did. Eventually, the portal faded away, indicating that her copycat had left the room. She would have to keep waiting.

Cate had no idea how long the wait would drag out. The day was far easier to track than the night. She could watch the sun shining in the windows, where it fell across the floor. She was fully aware of losing the day without being any closer to freedom. At moments, other windows of different shapes and sizes flashed before her in the darkness, fading as quickly as they arrived. Her impostor was doing its very best to stay away from anything that cast a reflection. Cate gave her credit – it was harder than it sounded. Yet, it managed to stay one step ahead. Cate never felt the pull to stand in front of the reflection; she could only imagine how relentless the other Cate was about moving in front of windows and mirrors as quickly as possible. She wondered if it had the same physical limitations that she did; she didn't have to imagine how exhausting such a task was.

But as the shadows grew longer, Cate felt her anxiety build. Night was coming again. It was almost a relief to feel something so human as dread. Of course, she would trade it for something along the opposite spectrum – delight or relief – but she didn't see much of that spectrum existing on this side of the mirror, especially as nightfall came closer.

She watched the mirror portal vanish almost completely again, feeling herself slip away with it. She didn't know if it was that she couldn't see herself, or if her physical being slipping away the longer she remained here. There was no way to know until it happened. All Cate could do was keep watch in the darkness and hope that her doppelgänger would slip up.

* * * *

By the time the sun shed light on the mirror's inner frame, Cate knew that hope was a far-flung idea. She had given in to curiosity and released who knows what on the world. It was going to disappear as the rest of them had. She didn't hold out hope that she would catch a glimpse of it with the coming day.

Her suspicions were painfully accurate. Cate sat in front of the mirror, looking out into Michael's quiet apartment and watched the sunshine crawl slowly across his floor from one side of the room to the other. She watched with a mixture of disappointment and apathy. She had exhausted her minuscule supply of hope on escaping this place, the last of it slipping away with her double, wherever it had gone.

She laid down, not even curious about what she rested on in the darkness. She no longer cared to know if she or anything had substance here when the light was absent. She didn't care what was in the dark if new light fell upon it. Cate laid down in a slow crumble until she no longer supported herself. She was almost positive that her face pressed to what passed for a floor here, but she didn't care. She couldn't cry; she couldn't even lose herself in the familiar comfort of discomfort. She was lost and ready to move on to whatever happened when reflections were abandoned by their hosts.

The universe, however, seemed to have other plans.

Another morning dawned, the sun finding Cate still crumpled and unmoving on the floor. With the arriving light, she was aware again of the subtle difference between her eyes being opened and closed. The darkness held her consciousness aware, but without stimulation. Like being trapped in a sensory deprivation chamber, if she could go on for eternity in this void, she felt that her mind would abandon her eventually.

She closed her eyes and stared off into the formless expanse behind her eyelids, opening them only when the light dimmed. It was so smooth, so gradual, yet she saw it and sat up as if it had been the most alarming event ever.

Perhaps in a way, it was, but it was only a cloud passing in front of the sun. She felt the hopelessness creep up on her again, allowing herself to give in, her tears almost coming only to recede like an unbidden tide.

Slowly, her body slipped back down to the dark floor, her mind listlessly drifting to strange curiosities. She dragged her palm, then her fingers, and finally her nails along the floor, surprised to see that she brought up nothing with them. No dirt, no bruises, not even pressure marks. There was no transference to speak of. The floor was and was not there at the same time, the same as she imagined herself: both trapped somewhere and nowhere simultaneously.

Cate shut her eyes, trying to drift off into the opaque formless wasteland before her, imagining it to be a better sentence than her current one when the light dimmed again. She started and then held herself, best not to put her hope into another selfish cloud.

She could see the light dim again, quickly, and before she could decide to react, an almost forgotten sense activated. In the soundless solitude beyond the mirror, her ears had become useless. This sound, however muffled and obscured, was like a scream and she stood up, pressing herself against the mirror.

"Cate!"

She couldn't see him, but she knew it was not her imagination. She pounded against the surface, trying to scream but nothing but a whisper came from her lips, no matter how loud she tried to yell. There was a strength that came through her desperation; a limitless supply of energy as long as she knew Lucas was somewhere nearby. She continued to pound on the surface of the portal, trying to cry out, fruitless as it might seem.

"Cate?"

He called as he moved through the apartment, sure to come back through, passing the mirror one more time – but would he see her? Could he? She shook the thought and continued, desperate to be heard, to be found.

When she finally saw him, he was moving quickly in the opposite direction. Lucas hadn't even bothered to look at the mirror. He rolled right past it, his stride long and determined in the mere moments he was within view. She knew by looking at him that he was already focused on his next step – mentally, he was already out of the apartment. She pounded on the mirror, her face feeling hot and flush for the first time since she crossed over, bodily throwing herself against the surface, hoping to make any kind of impact at all.

She pressed against the glass, willing herself to see around the corner, silently cursing Lucas and Michael for how they placed the mirror, but they couldn't have known – no one could have known. Her thoughts wandered back to Harriet, who had lived with this thing. How long had it waited, sitting in her bedroom, lonely and desperate? And even though it started with Cate, she couldn't help but wonder now why it came back for her when it had already taken Michael. Or was the thing in her reflection always after her? Had another someone else taken Michael? How many were out there in the world now, running around in bodies that weren't theirs? Where had they all gone?

She felt herself sliding down the surface, her body giving up on her again as the questions weighed her down.

She stared at the floor, pitying herself and her predicament. She didn't know how long she sat in her fugue before she noticed him. If the darkness hadn't stolen her voice, she might have cried out in surprise. Instead, she could only shuffle back, register what she saw before her, and scramble back to the portal again.

Lucas crouched in front of the mirror. His fingers were pressing delicately on the surface of the glass as if he were touching her. His eyes never met hers, but they were searching beyond the reflection, trying to peer into the world she was trapped in. Over and over, his lips repeated her name.

Cate stared out at him, her fingers tracing his; her eyes never leaving his, hoping for one more moment shared between them again. One hand pressed against the mirrored surface the entire time, supporting her, subconsciously fighting imprisonment still.

They remained separated by a barrier that, on one side, could well be as thick as any wall, and on the other as easily penetrated as silence. Yet neither could pass through their given side. Cate didn't move but found herself pressing harder and more bodily against the surface, her fingers tracing the space that once occupied his own movements. Lucas had since resigned himself to the floor, his legs folded under him as he tried to conceive a way of opening the mirror. Cate had a fleeting understanding that he had no proof she was trapped inside, only faith, but part of him seemed to know. He seemed to believe finally, or at least he convinced himself that he did.

THIRTY-FIVE

Lucas exhausted his last possibility. Hope had abandoned him, certain that wherever Cate was, she was far out of reach. He thought perhaps there would be a clue at Michael's apartment. There was no sign of her, no clue. She had disappeared, which led him to believe it had something to do with the mirror. Part of him still didn't grasp anything that was happening, but the unexplained had already overwhelmed the rational. It was time to go with the flow.

He left the hospital and immediately went to their apartment, hoping against hope, but other than some strewn clothing in the bedroom, there was no trace of Cate. He rushed to Michael's, the last place they'd been together, where the letter said she'd be. He ran around the small apartment, desperate to find her without having to go near the mirror.

In the end, he had no other choice.

He prodded at the mirror, looking for signs of change. He was afraid to cause it harm now. When it was something he didn't believe in, it made more sense to destroy it. Now that it was his last connection to Cate, wherever she was…

The light of the room changed, as it often did as twilight fell. It was a gradual change, and Lucas never really noticed until it was too late. Too dark to see clearly, but still light enough that people convinced themselves that it was adequate. Lucas realized he had no idea how long he'd been sitting there, wallowing and frustrated. He'd stared off into nothing and allowed himself to sink slowly into his desperation.

He looked at himself in the mirror; his eyes were red and dark, angry and exhausted. He thought he saw something else behind his eyes, then he realized he actually did. Leaning in, looming within a breath of the mirrored surface, he stared. There, behind his reflection, was another face. It was Cate, but it wasn't. It had to be her, yet she looked hollow, empty. She looked like a caged animal that would never taste freedom again. She was pressed against the glass, all but sleeping.

"Cate? Cate! Wake up!"

He banged on the glass, his open palm pounding as he yelled, his own voice ringing in his ears as he pressed his face right against the surface. She had to hear him, had to see him there – and she did.

Their eyes locked in the same joyful desperation that their fingers found. They could overlap, but they could not entwine. Separated by the paper-thin layer that kept one in and one out, they continued to try, sharing the hope and disbelief of the moment. Neither could hear the other, their voices swallowed by whatever power within the barrier truly separated them. Each reflected the other's light in their eyes: that it was a relief to both of them, knowing they'd found and been found, but it was still so bittersweet. It was clear that Cate had no more of a solution to penetrating the barrier than he did, and they couldn't even talk through it. But here they were, and they still had each other.

The sun, however, had not taken notice of these two lost souls reunited and continued on its course across the sky and over the horizon. It happened before anything could be said, or reacted to. In one moment, Lucas's tears streaked his face as he looked into Cate's eyes. In the next, he was staring back at himself, crying and confused as she was taken from him again without warning.

From Cate's side of the barrier, she only saw him looking sadly into her eyes, and then looking everywhere else desperately. Whatever veil had given them this moment had been revoked. Though she could see Lucas, she was cut off; she was alone again, the darkness creeping in once more.

THIRTY-SIX

For two more days, Lucas kept watch in front of the mirror. He didn't eat, he barely slept, he ignored his phone. Always waiting for some glimpse of Cate, and always rewarded for that handful of minutes at twilight. Although, as the two days stretched out before her, Cate didn't see it as much of a reward. She had already seen the effect of obsession on his face. The light was leaving his eyes, both literally and figuratively. He was starving himself before her and appeared to be utterly oblivious to his own reflection – even though he stared into it most of each day. She tried to convey her concerns through the glass, but he didn't seem to understand.

Two days passed, and he could only stare into the glass, caressing shapes into the barrier between them until she disappeared behind his reflection again. Then he would lash out in anger until he nearly broke the mirror, at which point he would recede into himself, and Cate would take her place on the opposite side of the glass and feel herself fade into the darkness for another night.

It was getting worse; Cate could feel it. Even with the lights on in Michael's apartment, spilling over into the mirror, Cate would still fade away in the early hours, feeling ghostlike herself, all thought and no form. Each morning she would return, but there was less substance to her; something was missing. She wondered if she was starving too, but without hunger pangs to measure it with. She knew she must be exhausted, but she couldn't really sleep either. The darkness was taking everything, a little at a time.

Another day began, Lucas appearing as distant and absent as she felt. He would fade in and out throughout the day, each time as if he'd been resuscitated. Swallowing air by the lungful, his eyes darting to the window to make sure he hadn't missed his moment. Cate couldn't watch him do this much longer. She knew that if she didn't go first, he would slip away right in front of her. What was the point to that? She could at least save him.

Cate watched the sunlight crawl across the room with growing tension, practically counting the minutes. Lucas came alive like a marionette, and she knew the time had come for her to be the stronger one.

She came close to the mirror, smiling softly. Lucas

pressed his hand against the glass, and for a moment, Cate wondered if this is how they would act if one of them were in prison – this painful separation where they could share their love and their emotions but nothing else. She knew that she couldn't live that way and that he, loving and dedicated as he was, shouldn't either.

Cate took a step back from the mirror, and Lucas stopped. He looked upset, confused. He started to speak, and though she could make out the croak of his weakening voice, she couldn't understand what he was saying. She looked over her shoulder into the dark, and he stood quickly on weak legs. His eyes were wild, his movements desperate. Lucas shook his head as he grabbed the mirror frame in both hands. She could hear the cry as he screamed at her, the words less important than their meaning: Don't go.

She put her fingers to her lips, blowing him a kiss and looked away, unable to take much more of the sadness weighing on what was left of her heart and soul. Taking another step back, Cate turned, moving further into the darkness until she could no longer hear him, could no longer see the portal where he stood crying. She walked until she felt the oppressive dark pressing in on her and knelt.

This seems like as good a spot as any.

Cate sat in the dark, almost relieved that she couldn't cry. She tried not to think about all the things that she would miss: Lucas, Rachel, Mabel, the bookstore, Sebastian – especially Sebastian. She would miss lazy Sundays and coffee – she might miss coffee as much as Sebastian if she were completely honest with herself. She closed her eyes, or at least she thought she did, but it was impossible to tell this deep in the darkness. She knew she wouldn't have to miss anything for much longer.

Cate wondered what it would be like to die in this realm. Would it really be dying, or would she disappear? Perhaps she would simply dissolve into the darkness, like so much smoke.

Dissolving would have to wait. Her reverie was interrupted by a crack of thunder ripping through the silent dark. A report so sharp and loud in the stillness that she was fully aware of ducking down and clamping her hands over her ears. She heard another whipcrack erupt in the darkness; a sliver of light split the void as it raced past her, deeper into the abyss. She turned, not sure what it meant, but almost certain that it had come from the mirror itself. She reached out, her fingers weaving through the light, making them glow and thinning the darkness around her. Her other hand shielded her eyes as she raced back, following the shimmering sliver. As she ran, a soft drumbeat thumped in her chest; she pushed herself harder. She needed to know what had happened, what it meant.

Maybe it's a way out!

She could practically feel herself as she ran. The light

grew brighter, almost warm on her skin as she approached the flood. Her thoughts crept to tunnels of light, but she hardly slowed her pace until the light was cut off from her.

She stopped, her heart breaking as the light vanished. She couldn't even see the portal that should have been in front of her. Was it gone as well?

"Cate?"

She couldn't have heard it, yet was sure she did. All at once, she realized that she heard it in that same strangled way that she could hear her own voice.

Here, on this side of the mirror...

As if he could see her brow creasing in question, Lucas stepped to the side, the light cutting through the darkness once again. She wanted to cover her eyes, she could feel pain from the intensity, but she didn't dare take her eyes off him. Running to him, wrapping her arms tight around, Cate couldn't be sure he was the real thing, but in the moment, it didn't matter. She ignored the doubt and held onto the moment as long as she could. His arms wrapped around her, and both bodies trembled against one another. Lucas held her arms and looked at her.

"We need to get out of here."

He pulled her along as she struggled with how he got in and, more importantly, how they were going to get out. Cate was disoriented, her eyes stinging as they ran together toward the light. She tried not to laugh at the metaphysical cliché they were taking part in.

Another sound quickly halted any consideration of laughter. It was an all-encompassing echo; a terrible noise like being torn in half, but in reverse. She didn't like the sound at all and felt Lucas urging her faster back the way he came. In the fraction of a moment, she understood everything and all but responded.

The shaft of light that had torn through the darkness, far beyond where she had traveled, now slipped past back them to its source point. Back to where Lucas came from. The sound, she could only guess, was whatever rip between the dimensions was being righted. With a snap of silence returning, the light disappeared.

Well, not *completely*.

There was a soft glow in the distance. They approached hand in hand, slow and resigned. When it was within sight, they plodded forward still, but they had reached the depth of surrender. Before them was the portal, the soft glow of morning rising in Michael's apartment. Between the portal and the morning was the other Cate and the other Michael. Lucas squeezed her hand in reflex, she responding in kind. Both stood on the other side of the mirror, stone-faced. They didn't bother gloating or controlling Cate. They regarded Cate and Lucas with something akin to curiosity, as if she was surprised to find both of them there, or perhaps to find them together.

Cate's duplicate stepped forward, studying the glass carefully. It traced a finger down the center in jagged angles.

Lucas squeezed Cate's hand again, and she knew that his way back through was gone.

The other Michael stepped forward, straightening a piece of fabric and stretching it across to the other Cate. Together, their eyes moved to the top of the mirror.

Cate leapt to the glass; her hands pressed against it. She knew she couldn't be heard through the glass, so she didn't bother trying to speak through it. She only mouthed the words that she wanted to say.

Please don't do this.

But her double could only regard her with the curiosity of an animal, one that couldn't process human compassion. Whether it was the words themselves or the nature of the request that was denied, Cate would never know. She saw no recognition in those eyes – only a foreign gaze looking back from a face she knew so well.

The cloth went over the top of the mirror smoothly, blocking out the light completely.

She could feel Lucas take her shoulders in his hands, turning her. He pressed his face against hers as she enveloped him in her arms. Together, they sank down onto whatever surface was beneath them and held each other tight.

In the absolute dark, Cate found she could neither hear nor speak; she tried to talk to Lucas, but nothing came. All she could do was keep her arms around him and hold on as he tightened his embrace around her, keeping her as close as possible. It was conceivable that he too was trying – and failing – to communicate, and this was the only way he could find to do so.

As time moved in its liquid, shifting way, Cate found she could no longer decipher its passage. She couldn't be sure they were still human, or what they might have become in the darkness. She knew Lucas was still with her; she could feel him. It wasn't fingers or caresses she felt, but a presence. A warmth within herself. Even though she could no longer feel herself in this place, or his body beside her, she knew he hadn't gone. His love held her close as hers held him and she knew, wherever they were drifting in the dark, that love would keep them together.

THE END

A Word from the Author

If you enjoyed this book – or, really, any book at all – please review it on all of your favorite merchant and social media sites. Or anywhere you can find it. If you can't find it somewhere, ask them to carry it. Readers are an author's lifeblood. They bring reviews, which bring more attention – and more readers – and encourage us to do what we do: keep writing.

If you would like to keep in touch, you can find me at:

www.happierthoughts.com

Most importantly though: Thank you.
For being a reader, and for taking a chance on me. I hope you enjoyed reading this as much as I enjoyed creating it.

- Andy

ACKNOWLEDGEMENTS

Bailey Lockwood kept me sane and worked magic as she always does: wrangling words and herding verbs. In general, making me sound far more competent than I actually am. Without her, this jumbled mess of words would never be fit to print.

Brian Ritson reached into my mind and pulled out the perfect cover for this story. His artistry is only matched by his friendship, of which I am eternally grateful.

You can view his portfolio at:

brianritson.wixsite.com

I also want to thank some amazing beta readers:

Marlene Bushouse	Sydney Bushouse
Chad Lee Erway	Amber L. Fuller
Melissa Kramer	Ryanne Nichols
Diana Kathryn Plopa	Judy Rushlow
Paul Spence	Sarah Standish

Writing is a lonely job, but it can't be done alone.
Thank you, one and all.

ABOUT THE AUTHOR

Andy Lockwood is a writer, artist, dreamer, and horror enthusiast. He got his start in screenwriting and filmmaking, where he rekindled his obsessive love of storytelling.

He is the author of two novels: *Empty Hallways*, and *House of Thirteen*; a 12-part serial, *At Calendar's End*, and is a regular contributor to horror anthologies. He is always at work on another piece of writing, whether it is a novel, a story, or something else entirely.

When not lashed to the keyboard, he buys books he does not have time to read, and delves into mediums he has no time to fully explore, but dabbles in them anyway.

He lives in Michigan with his amazingly talented and entirely-too-supportive wife, a brood of cats, and a misguided idea of what it means to be an adult.

More information about his books, his thoughts, and his random adventures are neglectfully curated at his website:

www.happierthoughts.com